Where Hope Is Found

by
Kait Reza

**PublishAmerica
Baltimore**

© 2008 by Kait Reza.
All rights reserved. No part of this book may be reproduced, stored in a retrieval system or transmitted in any form or by any means without the prior written permission of the publishers, except by a reviewer who may quote brief passages in a review to be printed in a newspaper, magazine or journal.

First printing

All characters in this book are fictitious, and any resemblance to real persons, living or dead, is coincidental.

PublishAmerica has allowed this work to remain exactly as the author intended, verbatim, without editorial input.

ISBN: 1-60672-143-7
PUBLISHED BY PUBLISHAMERICA, LLLP
www.publishamerica.com
Baltimore

Printed in the United States of America

Where Hope Is Found

Chapter One
Justice Clarks

"Out! I want you out of my house now!" Mr. Allen screamed at the top of his lungs. It was all he could do not to grab the figure slumped on the porch with her head in her hands and throw her off his property himself. He'd had it with this girl. She had been with them for a month, another poor foster child that his wife felt needed a home. His home. It wasn't that he hated sharing his home with homeless children. Oh no that wasn't it. It was the problems that came with the kids. In this case, Justice Clarks. She was trouble! Worse than trouble! With all of her fighting and drinking, the girl was a ship wreck! An absolute terror to be around. Her drinking problem was what had started his rage today. The night before she had come home completely drunk. Justice had caused such a noise that Mr. Allen and his wife awoke with a start. They came running into the den, to find that Justice had knocked over furniture. When confronted, Justice began to punch the air in front of him and lash out with her long legs. She went crazy knocking over everything in her path. She finally stopped when she got to her room. All the foul things she had slurred to him that night still stayed with Mr. Allen. Justice screamed about how bad her life was and how she wanted to die.

She told him that she would kill them if they came near her. Although he knew that the drunken girl couldn't even walk in a straight line if she wanted to, it bothered him that she would make a threat like that. Last night had been the last straw...Justice had to go. In the past month she had broken every rule they could think of enforcing. She snuck out at night, and stole from his wife, swore at him, refused to get up in the morning, smoked in the house, and the one he hated most...came home at night as drunk as could be. Justice also had about as bad of a temper as you could imagine. Nothing was spared her wrath when she was mad. Whatever was closest to break at the time got it bad! Most of the foster children they housed were bad, but Justice blew them all away. She was too much for him, his wife, and their house. She had to go.

"Justice I want you to stay out here until they pick you up." Mr. Allen grumbled.

Justice began to walk into the house.

"Where the heck do you think you are going? You stay right here, and don't move! Don't you dare step foot in my house missy or I'll call the cops to come pick you up instead like I should have last night!"

"I'm going to get a drink of water and if I hear you scream at me like that again, I'll throw this chair into your head, and show you what my headache feels like." Justice snarled.

"Well it's certainly not my fault that you have such a massive hang over. I don't get drunk like you do and destroy other people's houses!"

The troubled teen just rolled her light brown eyes. She came out of the door, walked down the porch steps and down the long driveway that separated the house from the busy street.

"Where are you going now? Get back here! Hey!" Protested Mr. Allen.

Justice smirked, but didn't even turn around. Let the old guy scream his lungs out. She wasn't about to wait around for the agency to pick her up. She could just hear Ms. Susan's voice again. She would be screaming at Justice for destroying, yet another perfect family for herself. Then she would ask that same demanding question, "Don't you want a family?" Well, Justice wasn't even sure that she *did* want one. Of all the countless homes where she had stayed, none were all that great. Justice had turned 16 a few days ago and she had already been in well over 60 homes in her teenage years. That was how bad she had become. Why she hadn't ended up in some mental home, she had no clue. All she knew was that not much was in store for her. Especially now. She had 2 more years until she could legally live on her own. Justice lived for the day she turned eighteen and could rid herself forever of the constantly nagging adoption agency. With only two years to go, Justice seriously doubted that she would find a decent home that could with stand her.

She walked along the narrow sidewalk lined with pretty little houses. The sun was bright, and the day was getting hot. Justice swept her long, straight, jet-black hair into a ponytail. Her faded jeans became increasingly uncomfortable as the morning grew hotter. She pulled at her peach tank-top trying desperately to cool herself off. She started to worry that her fair skin would burn, when she realized that she had bigger problems. Her head was pounding so hard that she thought her brain might just pop out of her skull. She had to sit down. As she neared the city that loomed ahead of her she figured that she would find an abandoned bench and rest. Justice thought that she should be accustomed to the massive hang-over she always had the day after extensive partying. Sometimes the headaches were so bad it almost made her want to stop drinking or at least not drink as much. However, she realized that something had to keep her alive. If partying and getting drunk did the trick, then well...

"Justice."

Aw man, Thought Justice. The car that pulled over to the side of the road was all too familiar.

"Nice to see you Susan" Justice smirked.

"Yeah, I can tell you're thrilled. Get in now." Susan unlocked the door and watched as the tall teen climbed into the passenger side. When the door was closed Susan reminded, "seat belt."

Justice did her all too famous eye-roll and buckled up.

As Susan sped away, Justice waited for the lecture she always got. When Susan remained quiet, Justice said "I'm ready for the lecture."

Susan laughed besides her self. "Since you seem to have already memorized them, there is really no need for me to give you another one. Besides, they never seem to affect you at all."

"Phew, well at least I'm spared that fun little speech."

"However, I will say Justice Clarks that you are one heck of a mess, and I have absolutely no idea where to take you. I guess you know that nobody even wants to hear your name mentioned. I say, for a troubled teen, you are clearly infamous my dear."

"Yeah, well maybe that's the way I like it. Maybe I don't want to get stuck with another crummy foster family that really doesn't care sh..."

"Justice," Susan cut in. "You know how I feel about you swearing in front of me."

"All I'm saying is that nobody I ever stay with even cares about me. That's why there is absolutely no reason to stay friendly with adults. They don't care about the orphan teen."

Susan sighed. "I seriously doubt that you don't want a family. I think it's just that you are so hardened that you can't even feel anything anymore." She thought a moment, "Except anger."

Chapter Two
A Possibility?

Jane Carter sat at the kitchen table sipping her coffee, and contemplating her next move: convincing her husband that adopting a kid was a good idea. It wasn't that her husband didn't want another kid. It was just that he wasn't over Vanessa. Vanessa Lynn Carter. Their perfect angel that was snatched away from them three years ago by an aggressive cancer. When Jane closed her eyes, she could still see Vanessa's thick auburn hair and excitable green eyes. A daughter that looked so much like herself, it sometimes was painful to look in her mirror. She always saw her daughter's face when she did. Vanessa's death had been rough on all of them. Jane really felt like she should adopt another child. But Bill Carter wasn't so sure.

"Jane, honey, I just don't think now is a good time. We have two kids, and Vance is just about to start college...I just don't see how this would work out. "Bill scratched his head and went to refill his coffee mug. "Plus, I just don't think the kids are ready for another sibling. Not after..." His voice trailed off as he thought of Vanessa.

"I know what you are thinking Bill, and I'm not saying we should adopt another kid to take away the pain of Vanessa, I just feel like...I don't know." She paused, "It just feels right. At least let's look into it."

"Jane I really don't know." Bill took a long sip of his coffee, and sat back down in his seat.

"Well let's pray about it then okay? If it's the right decision God will open the doors and if it's not, then I guess He will close them."

"Yeah, okay. I guess I could go with that." They both bowed their heads and prayed.

Later that day, Jane carter walked to her daughter's grave at the top of the hill. Her daughter had loved that hill when she was alive. In winter she was the first to go sledding on it, in autumn she would rake a pile of leaves from the trees that crowded it, make a big pile, and then jump in it. In summer she would rest in the shade and read. Whatever the season, Vanessa, always had a reason to go to her beloved hill. That was why Jane and Bill had arranged for the grave to be placed on the big hill, near their home. Jane knelt by the tombstone, and looked around at the trees. It was a hot day, but a cool breeze began to blow, and the leaves on the trees began to rustle. Jane smiled. It really was a pretty place. She began to sing. Singing just seemed like the right thing to do right now, just like adopting another kid was the right thing. Almost without realizing it, she began to talk, at first not really sure who she was talking to, but then decided that she was going to tell Vanessa. Whether or not she heard, it didn't matter.

"So Vanessa, Your father and I are thinking of adopting another kid. Not to replace you at all honey, I'm sure you understand that. I'm sure you wouldn't mind. You always did well when we adopted our first kid. Oh honey, I miss you. We all do. We are getting by, but everyday we think of you. I know

Valley misses you a lot. I know that you are in a beautiful place right now. I think if you had the chance to come back to this horrible planet you would choose not to. Heaven really must be a wonderful place." Jane laughed. But also wiped away some tears "I describe to Valley what I think heaven looks like. It makes her feel so much better to know that you are happy where you are now. "Jane paused, and looked around. She did this once in a while. It was her way of coping with the loss of her daughter. In her heart she knew that Vanessa couldn't hear her, but her mind wouldn't let go of her. "I loved you so much honey. I wish you could see this place right now. It's so pretty up here. The wind is blowing all the leaves around, and the sun is streaming down. Vanessa, I really want to adopt another child, but I don't know if I could stand another girl…other than you or Valley. "Jane Carter looked around again and then looked at her watch on her thin wrist." Well I had better go. I'll come up here again soon darling." Jane wiped away any excess tears and took a deep breath. She didn't know why she always put herself through this. She just knew that she had to. It kept her sane. Jane Carter walked down the big hill, and started her short trek home. She wondered if God would want her to adopt another child. Would He?

Chapter Three
Another Foster Home…NOT!

"What the heck!" Justice yelled. "Grrrr you can't place me with those old farts! I doubt they even have their driver's licenses any more…they can barely see, they are so old!"

"Justice." Susan warned.

"No. I refuse to go. You can't make me." Justice leaned back in the chair across from Susan's desk. They were back at the agency in Susan's office. "In fact if I say no, then the law says that I don't have to go. You know that. I'm sixteen now, I can choose where and when I want to go."

"Justice, let me remind you young lady that you don't have another place to go. You don't have an option. There is no where else for you to spend the next month and a half." Susan remained calm. She was all too used to Justice's outbursts. "You have to go to the O'Malleys; they're the only emergency foster home available. Besides, you don't have to stay there forever, only until we can find a better home."

Justice screamed. "I don't want to go! My life sucks! I don't need any of this." She got up.

"Justice you may not leave this room."

"Why not? The O'Malley's left already!"

"They are coming back for you Justice; they just need to fill out some paperwork." Susan took a sip from her plastic cup.

"Yeah you just think of everything don't you Susan? I think you like watching me get stuck in these sorry situations."

"That's not true Justice; I want you to find a home as bad as anybody. Believe me." Susan massaged her head, and repeated, "Believe me."

Justice was just about to argue when the old couple walked back in the room.

"Well Hello again. Justice was just telling me how she was going to behave." Susan smiled. The old couple, Susan, and Justice walked out of the tiny office, and into the main part of the building.

"Okay well, If you need anything here's my number," Susan handed the old couple a card with her name, number and the agency on it. "I will be calling to check up on things." She gave her a piercing look, "So Justice behave."

"Watch what happens." Justice replied.

"I mean it. "Susan warned. She smiled at the old couple. . "If anything comes up please don't hesitate to call. You really shouldn't have any problems." Susan clapped her hands together. "Well I guess that's all. Justice got your stuff?"

When the girl didn't reply Susan assumed she had everything. "Great, well I'll see you in a little over a month!"

The old couple drove really slow, and the elevator music they insisted on playing, was disturbing Justice greatly. She sat in the back of the old rickety car, and bounced along the bumpy road. The place they were going was in the middle of the country and among a whole bunch of old farm houses. Justice wanted to die. There was no way she could stand this place for over a month. No way at all. She had to escape...but how? Where would she go? Justice sighed, and closed her eyes.

"Something wrong dearie?" the old lady asked.

"No I just have a hang-over that's all." Justice replied with a smirk. She wanted to convince this old lady, and her husband that she was too much to handle.

"Oh." Was what the old lady said. Maybe she was hard of hearing.

They pulled up into a long driveway that worked it's way to a little house. Surrounding the house was a white picket fence. To Justice it looked like a little prison. What the heck was she going to do all night?

"We're home." Said the little old man. "Come on Barbara; let's show this young lady around." Two hours and twenty seven minutes later, they had looked at every rock and pebble, the land had on it. Justice was so completely bored out of her wits, that she asked if she could just go to her room and sleep.

The old couple looked at each other and asked if she would like to eat dinner first.

"Barb made her famous lentil stew." Hank (the old guy's name) said.

"Yeah I bet you'll like it darling'" Barb announced.

"Yeah, I bet I would but, uh, I am so tired I can't even eat." Justice lied.

"All right then dear your room is right there." Barbara pointed to a room at the end of the small hall that led out of the living room.

"Thanks." With that Justice walked down the hall to her new room, and closed the door.

As soon as the door shut, she started thinking of how she would get out of her current prison. There was a window in her room that she could climb through. She remembered seeing a gas station about a mile down the road from them. She could walk there, and call a cab to take her to town. Then she could try to find some of her friends, and they could all hang out or something. She just had to time it right. If the little old couple found out that she was gone before she made it to the gas station, then she would be done for. They would surely notify Susan, and then Susan would find her. Justice would be in so much trouble. What could they do to her? Thoughts of the mental hospital still lingered in her mind...

At 10:00 Justice figured that the old couple would most likely be asleep. She hadn't heard a sound coming from their little room. She crept to her bedroom door and opened it a crack. There was no sound in the little hall. She took a cautious step out the door, and closed it carefully. She grabbed her back-pack and slung it over her shoulder. The bag was her only companion. Justice opened the front door of the den and stepped out. The air was slightly chilly. She closed the door behind her with a gentle pull, and then headed down the driveway.

Half an hour later, Justice made it to the gas station. The lights were all out at the station, signaling that no one was there. Justice walked around the place a little. It almost seemed abandoned. Like everything else out here. Justice found much to her disappointment that the payphone was broken. So how was she going to call her friends?

She sighed. What now? She sat on a little bench to think. There was the obvious going back, but there was no way in the world Justice wanted to try to spend a month and a half inside a little picket fence. No way. So what other options were there?

If she only had a car to herself things would be good. Justice smiled. Well, there was one way out of this place. Wasn't there another gas station just a mile down the road? It looked like it was in much better shape than the one she was at now. She would look for a payphone. Twenty minutes later she found one near the gas station. Digging in her pockets for change Justice tried to remember the number.

Her friend had just recently gotten her license and would be more than happy to drive her to town. As Justice inserted the change necessary for the call, she thought about Lacee. Lacee didn't live that far from the gas station. She was recently adopted by a couple who lived near. They seemed nice enough. Justice dialed the number. Although Justice would never admit it, she envied Lacee. Lacee was so easy-going and eager to please. Everybody liked her. That was why Lacee now had a home and she was still an orphan. The phone began to ring. It rang four times before Lacee picked up. "Hello?" She said in a sleepy voice.

"Hey Lace, It's me Justice."

"Oh hi...Should I be wondering why you are calling so late? I mean it's almost midnight and I just got home from work an hour ago and was kind of asleep but..."

"Lace, I have a bit of a situation."

"Oh no." came the response, "Do I have to bail you out of jail or something?"

Justice laughed." No worse, I'm stuck in another foster home, in farm country, er, your country and I really want out. You wouldn't by any chance be able to give me a ride would you?"

Justice heard a deep sigh on the other end. Okay, so maybe Lacee wasn't jumping at the chance to give her a ride. "Look Justice, that's not such a good idea. Susan will kill you, if you run away again."

"Yeah I know, but I..." Justice paused. "I have to get out of here."

Lacee could tell that Justice was distressed. But she always was. Justice was never satisfied in one home or another.

"What if you get caught?" she asked.

"I won't. The couple I'm staying with are old. I left them a note for the morning saying that I went out for a run."

Lacee rolled her eyes. "Okay, well since you've already planned this entire thing out I guess I'll give you a ride."

"Yes!"

"On one condition."

Justice grew solemn, "What's that?"

"Don't tell anybody who you got the ride from okay? I want out of all your little crimes and punishments. Plus, if my new parents found out I snuck out to give you a ride. I would be in huge trouble."

"Alright."

"Okay, where are you calling from?"

"What looks like an abandoned gas station?"

"Yeah I know what you're talking about. I'll be over there in about five minutes okay?"

"Great thanks girl." Justice meant it with all her heart.

"Yeah, yeah." Lacee said as she hung up.

In slightly over five minutes, Lacee pulled up. "Sorry" she said, "I got lost in the dark."

"Yeah this place is really dark out here." Justice agreed as she climbed in the car.

"It's because we're so far from the city."

"Yeah, no lights." Justice mumbled.

"So Justice, when are you ever going to settle down?" Lacee asked.

"Probably never. At least not while I'm a teen."

"Doesn't being homless without a family really get to you?"

Justice looked out the window. "No one wants me."

Lacee laughed, "Yeah not with your destructive powers."

"No, but I'm serious Lace, I think even if I was good, nobody would want me. I'm too old."

"Yeah well, I wasn't exactly young when they adopted me!" Lacee exclaimed.

"Yeah but you just have this way about you that everybody likes."

"Well you know I believe there is somebody out there for everyone. Even you."

The car fell silent for a while, and Lacee cranked up the radio.

As Justice waved goodbye to her friend, the conversation they had whirled around in her head. Would she ever settle down?

Nah, probably not. Justice walked to her favorite bar to see if she could find her friends.

"Hey, I thought you were stuck in another foster home." Greg snickered as Justice joined him and his friends at their usual table.

"Yeah well, I got out." Justice answered not bothered by Greg's sarcasm.

"Whoa you got out again? How many times has that been this month? Twelve?" Asked Ryan who sat across from her.

"Fourteen actually."

Greg laughed.

"Hey Janet." Justice had known Janet for about as long as she could remember; Janet was the one who had introduced her to the group.

Janet gave an almost unnoticeable nod.

"What's up with her?" she asked Ryan as he scooted closer to her.

Ryan whispered "She just broke up with Rick, so she's not in the best of moods."

"Yeah well that was bound to happen. The guy was a jerk."

"Yeah well I know that, and you know that, but Janet…well, she didn't seem to see it." Ryan pointed out.

"Yeah well, it sucks for her, but I'm glad she doesn't have to deal with him anymore."

"Yeah me too." Ryan paused. "So why did you run away this time?"

Justice sighed. "I just didn't feel like staying. I was stuck with oldies and well…" Justice stood up and said "I'm going to go get a drink."

"Don't you think you've had enough of those lately?" Ryan asked.

"Not really." Justice answered truthfully. *Not enough to make her forget how bad her life was.*

"Kids we need to talk about something." Said Bill Carter as he sat on the sofa next to his wife. Vance and Valley were sitting across from them on lazy boys.

Whenever they had these kinds of meetings, something was always about to happen. Sometimes good, and sometimes very bad. Vance thought about one of the times three years ago when his parents announced that his sister Vanessa, probably wouldn't make it. That had been tough. Now as he listened to his dad try to come up with the right words, he got anxious.

"What I'm trying to say is that your mother and I have decided to…well if it's God's plan, we would really like to…"

"What dad?" Vance asked getting impatient.

"Sorry, I just don't want you to take this the wrong way."

"Why would we take it the wrong way daddy?" Asked Valley.

"What I want to say is." Bill stuttered more, so Jane picked up.
"We want to adopt another kid."
Vance and Valley just stared.
"Why?" asked Valley.
"Well, because." Jane started. "Because we believe that there is a little boy." She paused, "Or girl, that needs a home."
"Why can't they get another home?" Valley asked.
Bill scratched his head again. Whenever he was nervous or trying to get a point-across he always scratched his head. "Valley we want to be that home." Was all he decided to say.
"But I don't want another brother, and definitely not a sister." Valley announced decidedly. "Do you want another sibling Vance?"
"Val, I think mom, and dad are right. There are a lot of kids out there who need a home. I think we would be a good home for one of those kids." Vance looked at his sister trying to read her mind. Valley had taken Vanessa's death the worst, but it didn't mean that they were over her. He still wasn't over his younger sister's death.
"See Valley we don't mean to…" Jane tried to put it gently. "Replace Vanessa. We just feel like adopting another kid is the right thing."
" Well I don't." Valley pouted. At nine years old she was still the baby.
"It's not up to you Val." Her dad told her gently. "I know it will be hard at first, but I know that you will grow to love your new sibling."
Valley looked at him with her eyes determined. "No I won't."

"Yeah well, I'll see you guys later." Justice said, and walked with Janet to her car. She figured that she would just spend the night at her place. Janet was eighteen and had just moved into her own little apartment. Her roommate Karly was on vacation, so they didn't have to worry about waking her up at three in the morning.

As they walked to the parking lot, Justice couldn't help talking a little. "So I heard you had a rough day."

"Yeah, that's an understatement." Janet pushed her short blonde hair behind her ears. And searched for her keys in her purse.

"That's true. My day sucked too. "

"Really?" Janet asked without looking up. "Why, was it your foster family again?"

"Yeah pretty much…"

Janet swore. "Okay, I think I left my keys in the bar. I have to go get them."

"I'll go with you."

As the girls walked across the street, a police car stopped in front of them. Justice groaned when she noticed who the cop was. It was Officer Anders, the same cop who always brought her back to the adoption agency, every time she ran away.

"Uhhh I think I'm going to walk quickly, how about you?" Justice glanced at Janet.

"Is that…?" She pointed.

"Yeah." Justice practically ran across the street. She was just about to walk back into the bar when she heard.

"Justice Clarks."

When she turned around the cop smiled and said, "Fancy seeing you here, again."

"Yeah." Justice stood silently staring at the ground.

"I'm guessing you're not here with a guardian…am I correct?"

it was more of a statement, and Justice knew it. She also knew that there would be no point in lying about it. She had tried that once and it didn't work out too well.

"Hey how did you know?" Justice tried some humor.

The cop smiled but didn't say anything. Justice and Officer Anders had somewhat of a friendship. He would spy her on the street, the agency would call him and report a missing foster child, and he would catch Justice and send her back. It happened a lot. Oh she had tried all her tricks on him. Saying that her guardian was there. Even trying to convince him that her friends were her siblings. She had run, and she had fought. The girl would complain and complain about the people she had to live with. In the end though, she was always sent back to her home, only to go 'missing' again in a week or so. Lately it had been worse. Justice could sometimes get away with three days, before she was found. The girl was getting smarter. Her sneaking out became more frequent, and lately it had been nearly everyday.

The cop put his attention back on Justice. "Well I think you know the drill, hop in."

"Do I have to? You don't know the people I have to stay with! They're old and ugly…"

"Justice, I don't want to hear it. I'm sure they are awful, but I can't leave you without some kind of guardian."

"Can you just throw me in jail then?" Justice only half joked.

The cop laughed. "You don't mean that Justice. Anyway what happens now? Will you be put back with that family? If you are you'll probably be back out tomorrow night." He sighed. "What happens when school starts back up? Are you going to be this bad then?"

She didn't want to answer. "Yeah…. I don't know."

"Well get in, we'll see what your punishment will be this time."

Justice sighed and said "whatever." She gave Janet a hug and promised to call her as soon as she could. "Off to my doom." Justice groaned as they drove away. "Susan is going to kill me."

Chapter Four
Decisions

    Jane thought about the words her daughter had spoken hours ago. "I don't want another sibling." She had said. Would Valley ever get use to another kid in the family? Bill seemed to think so. Jane got up from her bed and went to the kitchen. She couldn't sleep, so it didn't matter if she made herself another cup of coffee. The whole adoption thing was a lot for the kids to handle. It wouldn't have been as bad if Vanessa had still been alive. Yet still, Valley may have been like that. Who could know? All she could think of was some little kid out there in need of a home. Maybe it was a little boy who was lonely and dreamed of a better life. Wouldn't their family be perfect for him? Surely Valley wouldn't mind him. Maybe that was the direction to lean… A little boy. Valley surely wouldn't think of him, like she would with another girl. Another girl would replace Vanessa in her little mind. But a boy who was younger than Valley herself, would be a whole new experience. It might actually be a good thing for Valley to become the older sibling. Yeah. A good thing. Jane liked the way this line of thinking was going. Tomorrow she would research and find out what kids were in need of homes. Of course they would foster the little boy first; to make sure everything went all right, but then… It would all work out. Somehow Janet knew that it would all work out. She picked her freshly brewed coffee up and poured some in a mug. Yeah it would all work out.

When Susan got to the office, Justice could tell that she had been awakened from a very good sleep. Justice was about to pay dearly. She couldn't even look Susan in the eye, for fear Susan would bore a whole through her own, with that angry glare. Susan looked at the cop first and said "Thank you Officer Anders. I'm sorry to make you drive all this way," She paused, "Again."

"It's no problem Susan, it's the end of my shift anyway."

"Gee thanks." Justice mumbled to him.

Susan redirected her gaze and Justice winced as it fell on her, "As for you…I can barely say your name I'm so mad!" Susan exploded. "How could you do this!" She added, "Again? "

"Well, I told you it wasn't going to work out! They can't handle me they're too old!" Justice defended herself.

"Do they even know that you are missing?" Susan demanded.

"Nope. I even wrote them a note for the morning. It said something about a morning run." Justice smiled. That wouldn't have worked on just any foster family. Maybe being watched by older people was a good thing.

"Why are you smiling? You're in big trouble Justice!" Susan continued, "What am I going to do with you? Huh?"

At this point the cop excused himself saying that if they needed him for anything to call. He gave an encouraging wink at Justice. No matter what the girl did. He felt some pity for her.

Some of the people she stayed with were unique individuals. Unique meaning, sometimes hard to manage.

"Justice this is getting really serious. "Susan rubbed her head. She was getting another headache from this girl.

"Well too bad. All the people you put me with suck. I can't stand it anymore."

"So what do you want to do about it?" Susan asked

Justice could actually feel some tears well up, before she quickly blinked them away. "I'm going to kill myself."

✱ ✱ ✱

Jane and Bill had just told the agency about their decision to adopt another kid earlier that day. They said that they would be willing to adopt any kid who needed a home, but they would really like a little boy. The lady seemed to know of a few and said that she would get back to them soon. So the Carter's decided to invite their church bible study group over, and ask for their prayer. They wanted to share some things with the group, and get some feed-back from them. They were here now, at six o clock, and were in the living room ready to begin. Jane carried a food tray with, cookies, and coffee, and set it down on the table. Bill got their bibles and they got ready to begin.

Chapter Five
The Phone Call

What Justice said last night really bothered Susan. They had decided to just spend the night at the office, and call the O'Malleys in the morning, well Morning had come and gone. The O'Malleys hadn't even noticed the note at first, and when they did they didn't suspect anything other than what Justice had written. Okay so maybe they weren't the best place for Justice to be. How was she to know that? Justice could be such a pain. What would she do with her now? Especially since she announced that she wanted to kill herself. Susan racked her brain of all the possible people she could call. None seemed to come to her mind. She had tried everyone. Everyone. Nobody could stand Justice, and the ones that hadn't had her yet learned from the ones that did and quickly discovered that they didn't want her near them. Susan remembered the first time she had met Justice. Justice was about four years old. She had been really talkative back then. She was a sweet kid. Susan had heard some of how Justice had come to the agency, but she couldn't remember all the details. She went to the filing cabinet, and looked for "Clarks." She came across it. The folder looked like it had been flipped through a lot. Most of the time Susan would tell the foster parents a little about the child they would be looking after, but for Justice she simply said that she had been passed around a lot and that's why she was such a terror. It was better they didn't know everything.

Susan opened the folder. She read, and re-read the whole thing. What she saw written there was terrible.

After a while, she closed the folder and walked back to see Justice. Justice was sitting in her big office chair and spinning. She had a pair of old headphones on, and even from the distance Susan was standing from the office, she could hear the rock music blaring. The only thing that seemed to content Justice.

Susan stepped into the office. After getting all of the angry things out last night, she had a little more compassion for her today. Susan pulled a Hershey's bar from her desk and tossed it to Justice. "Here want it?" Chocolate was every girl's comfort, even for Justice. Justice nodded her thanks and began to eat the soft chocolate.

"Listen Justice. We need to talk." Susan began.

Justice continued to ignore her.

"Justice please listen…"

Justice was now playing air guitar and swinging her head back and forth.

"Justice!" Susan yelled.

Still no answer.

Susan got up and ripped the headphones off her head.

"Hey those are mine!" Justice yelled automatically.

"I need you to listen to me, and then I'll give them back, I promise." Susan said, feeling like she was talking to her little niece when she turned the TV off for dinner.

Justice sighed, "Oh let me guess you are in so much trouble, blah,blah, blah, and I can't believe you, blah, blah, blah. And now I'm gunna place you in this other family, and then blah…blah…blah."

"Are you done?" Susan asked.

"Yeah mostly." Susan wanted to smack the girl, but she remembered what Justice's papers said about what she had been through. Sometimes it was easy to forget compassion. She decided to let her comments slide.

"Actually I wanted to talk about last night."

Justice stared at the wall and answered, "Yeah well duh, that's no surprise."

"No Justice. Do you really want to kill yourself?" Susan finally asked. Justice sat up in the big office chair.

"Maybe. I mean my life isn't about to get any better."

"You don't know that." Susan offered.

"Yeah I do. At least with you on the job. "

Susan gave her a look.

"Oh come on! Look at me!" She jabbed a finger at herself. "I'm a sixteen-year-old that's been tossed ungratefully from home to home. Isn't it obvious to you yet? People don't like to adopt older children."

"Well, some of them do, your own friend was adopted at sixteen, and…"

"And what? What are you trying to say?" Justice cut her off,. "That it's just me? I just happen to be the one nobody wants?"

"You know why they don't want you! You have a temper!"

"Well I can't change who I am!" Justice's voice rose.

"But you could change your temper!" Susan shot back.

"Why? What would that do? I'd still get stuck with another stupid foster family."

"If you just gave the families a chance Justice…."

"I have. I've given families my all, and gained nothing but pain in return."

Susan stopped. There was no point. Justice was too hardened.

"Justice if you won't calm down then there is only one thing left: you'll need to be hospitalized for psychological instability."

Justice laughed. It was a long hysterical laugh that made Susan squirm. "You mean some mental hospital?"

"I'm sorry," she frowned, "But I don't see the humor in that."

Justice wiped her now tearing eyes, "It's just that I knew you would throw me into that place someday. Even you can't stand me."

"We use to get along so well. What happened?" Susan sadly asked.

"I grew up, and learned the truth." Justice stood and walked out of the room. She called back,

"I'm gunna get ready for the mental hospital and you know, pack my toothbrush and skimpy accessories."

Susan released a sigh and tried once again to rationalize the situation. There must be another way. Something else for the girl. Suddenly the light when she remembered the call she had received just earlier that day. What was the name of the family? Susan went to her desk drawer and received the paper with the information on it. The family's name was Carter. She remembered the kind voice on the phone as Bill Carter explained that they would be willing to adopt any child that needed a home. They had said that they would love a little boy, but any child was welcome. Any child? Susan stared at the paper. Would she be cheating their kindness, if she handed Justice to them? What if the family couldn't stand her? Well that was pretty much a given. What if the family decided never to adopt again, because of the terror Justice bestowed on them? Then she would have ruined it for another child. So many problems. Yet... what other choice did she have? Justice needed a home. What else would she do with the girl? She really didn't want to send her away to a mental facility. Maybe she could ask the family to watch her for just a week, and if Justice was too much of a terror...she would take her. Susan nodded to herself. It would be Justice's last chance, and then she would feel like she gave the girl her all. Susan picked up the phone and dialed the number. The phone began to ring. It rang and rang, and Susan was just about to hang up when she heard, "Hello?"

The phone rang, and Bill Carter rose to get it. He excused himself from the group. They had just finished their study, and were now swallowing refreshments.

The phone continued to ring. "I'm coming, I'm coming." Bill picked up the phone. "Hello?"

Bill paused and the placed his hand over the receiver and called for his wife, "Jane can you come here?"

Jane excused herself from the group, and walked to the kitchen where her husband stood with the long cord of the phone twirled between his fingers. His hand was over the receiver as he said, "Hon, this is the adoption agency. They want to know if we will take a sixteen-year-old girl for a week."

Jane's eyes grew big. A sixteen-year-old girl? That wasn't what she had expected when she had agreed to adopt any kid. Still, this girl needed a home. How bad could a week be? "Yeah, say that we will ." Jane looked at Bill with confidence, "She needs a home for a week, and so she shall have one."

Bill spoke onto the phone, "Yeah, we'll take her. When do we pick her up?"

Now it was Bill's eyes that turned big, as he hung up the phone.

"What's wrong?" Jane asked.

"Nothing. We pick Justice up tomorrow."

"Justice?"

"That's her name."

"Well let's spread the news to everyone," Jane exclaimed enthusiastically.

"Yeah and I guess we'll tell the kids tomorrow."

"Yeah" Jane agreed. "When they're awake," She didn't add, "And when Valley is in a good mood."

As they walked back into the living room, where the rest of their guests were, Bill said to Jane. "That lady on the phone sounded pretty desperate. She wouldn't stop apologizing either. She acted as if she were about to unload some kind of huge burden upon us. "

"Well Bill, asking us to watch a child might very well be a big burden. To foster a sixteen-year-old however, well that might be a bit of an effort."

The couple excitedly told the group their news. Little did they know of the terror that awaited them, when they finally met Justice Clarks.

Telling the kids the next morning, was one of the most stressful things that a mother ever had to go through! Thought Jane. They were now on their way to the agency, but the car remained silent. Jane thought of all the other possible ways that she could have broken the news to her kids. There weren't any others that she could think of. They would just have to be supportive. Vance seemed okay with the idea for the most part. He was just concerned about his room. After assured that he would get to keep it, he fell silent and seemed not to worry about it anymore. But Valley… She threw such a fit! Jane and Bill didn't even know that their daughter was capable of throwing one such as that. She was especially mad, when she found to her horror that Justice would be rooming with her for the week.

They had simply told her that she was just going to have to accept Justice. It was only for a week. Jane just hoped that Valley wouldn't show her disappointment to Justice. That was the last thing the poor girl would need. Although, she was sure that Justice was accustomed to rejection, since she was still unadopted. The closer they got to the agency, the more Jane knew that she was doing the right thing. Or at least going the right direction. The rest of the ride, Jane thought about the things they would introduce Justice to. Susan had called again that morning to make sure they were all set to pick Justice up. There was only one thing that worried Jane a little. Susan said that Justice had been in a lot of foster homes lately. She had said that the girl had a bad temper, and that she had scared a lot of people away. However, Susan did admit that some of the homes that Justice was placed in, were not very welcoming ones. Jane thought she may have just said that to give them a little more confidence in Justice. How bad could a sixteen-year old possibly be?

Chapter Six
"Meet the Carters"

    Justice once again got her things together, and waited rather impatiently for the family to come pick her up. What happened now? Justice didn't know. What if she couldn't deal with this family? Would she really be sent to a mental hospital? She would like to think that perhaps Susan was just trying to scare her into being good... but she just didn't know. Susan had sounded so angry the other night. She tried to imagine what a mental place was like. Restricted schedules, weird food, no smoking, strange doctors and possibly crazy people running down the hall. Not a place she really wanted to be. Maybe she should give these people a try. Justice began to think. She couldn't let Susan know though. Otherwise he would think that she had won. Justice couldn't have that. No way!
    "Hey Hun. I know that it's hard moving around so much, but you are just going to have to make the most of this one." Susan walked by and patted Justice's shoulder. "They just pulled up and are about to come in. Why don't we go out and meet them?" It wasn't really a question.
    So Justice stood with as little enthusiasm as possible, and followed Susan sullenly out of the little office. The hallway that

separated them from the front of the building, seemed like an endless stretch. Even time seemed to slow for just that moment. The moment that Justice was to see her new home. *Get ready for a new challenge.* She told herself.

They reached the end of the hall, and Susan pushed the door that kept them from the main office. Susan's face turned into a big smile as she greeted the family that sat in a long row, waiting for Justice. A little girl with brown hair, and bright blue eyes, and looked about age 9, gave Justice a long piercing stare, before she returned her attention to Susan. She gulped. That was one judgmental look. The son, who looked much like his sister, gave Justice a little more ease. He smiled slightly. Justice didn't know what to do, so she smiled back.

"So Carters, this is Justice Clarks. "Susan was saying. Justice heard the acquaintance speech a little too much. "… And Justice, this is the Carter family." Justice decided to play along for the mean time. She was still in shock that she was being put into a family with other kids. She couldn't actually remember a time when she had foster siblings. This was really different. "Hi." Justice smiled. *Whoa did I just smile? I'm really getting good at this pretending. It almost felt real.* She shook it off.

A lady with Auburn hair and green eyes stood up and extended her hand to Justice. "Hello Justice. We have really been looking forward to meeting you. I'm Jane, and this is my husband Bill, and my two kids Vance, and Valley."

Justice stood for a second, looking at all the faces. Was she really supposed to get to know, and love all of them?

"I'm sure you will all get along fine. "Susan said with a too happy smile.

Justice wanted to laugh. Was Susan seriously suggesting that she would decide to get along with them? Then the other part of her mind was pressing her to just try to make things go right.

What was better than a perfect family, and a secure place to live? Plenty of things. Justice knew that she was in charge of the situation and with that in mind, she stepped out of the walls of a building that was just waiting to snatch her back up. She walked into the morning, with the sun shining encouragingly.

The Carters were careful to show her the little town, so she would feel more at home. Justice was almost certain that it was Jane Carter's idea. The tall lady always seemed so energetic and ready to make you feel welcome. Justice was to her dismay, already starting to like her a little. She seemed nice. A lot could change an adult's mind though. She wanted to see what Jane would do if she caught her at some big party. Would it faze her, or would she be expecting it because she had Vance? Justice looked at the tall boy sitting next to her in the red station wagon. He didn't really look much like a party boy she decided. He was clean cut, and at the moment had a very serious look on his face, as he gazed out the window. Maybe he was thinking about all the difficulties of having a foster kid in the home.
"Oh Justice this is our church. "Jane said as they drove the car around the parking lot. "Bill is the Pastor here, so as you can imagine we spend a lot of time at this place. "
Oh great, thought Justice. She was stuck in a preacher family. No wonder Jane was being so nice. Now she was probably doing her pastor wife duty, and trying to lure her with kindness into their religion. Well it was a nice try but she wasn't going to crack that easy. She would make sure that Jane knew that very soon.
However, Justice didn't know that they would live so close to the church, and within walking distance. Did that mean that they would have to go to church all the time? Would they force her to come along? Justice knew that she was in for a ride.

The home she saw was a decent size, at least big enough for the Carters, and perhaps a guest or two. It looked pleasant enough, Justice decided. There was a pretty flower garden in the front yard and a big oak tree stood in the middle. An old wooden swing hung from one of it's branches. The car pulled into the long driveway and came to a stop outside of the garage. Everybody hopped out, and headed for the front door. Although Justice was trying to seem reserved she couldn't help complimenting the garden as they passed by it. Jane had looked genuinely pleased that she had taken notice. When Justice stepped through the front door, she found herself in a warm living room. The walls were painted a light yellow, and the whole room gave off a slightly country look. They took her through the living room and down a hall into the kitchen. To the left of the kitchen was a dining room, with a wonderful chandelier hanging over the long table. It looked like it was used maybe twice a year…Christmas and Thanksgiving. Most of the time they ate at the kitchen table, Justice was told.

Upstairs Justice was led to her room. Jane approached the door, and turned the knob very gently, like somebody could actually be in there, and not expect her to come in. The room was painted pink, with beautiful long silky shades that seemed to be blowing in the breeze. Justice saw that the breeze was let in by a large window that was opened slightly. There was a canopy over the single twin bed, and it matched the curtains. A bright pink bedspread, and pink and white pillows were a match. All the furniture in the room was white including a white fluffy chair that Justice longed to sink into. She had to admit that she had never been offered such a beautiful room in any of the other homes she had been in. In fact, it had always been the opposite. She was usually given a guest room that had ugly wall paper, or was given in extra mattress to sleep on in another room of the house. This room was very pretty. Maybe a little pink for Justice's tastes, for she had never really considered herself much of a girly-girl, but it was nice.

"Well I hope you'll be comfortable here," Jane said.

"It's a very pretty room." Justice announced as she circled the room, examining the very pink walls.

Jane laughed and winked as she headed for the door. "Don't let the pink get to you."

Justice smiled, then turned around and started to unpack. She placed her few sets of clothes into the white dresser that had a pretty white-framed mirror attached to the top of it. Her dark reflection looked back at her. Her black hair hung straight, and long. Her wispy bangs were pushed to the side of her face, and her hazel eyes looked tired. Dark bags hung low, tell-tale signs that she hadn't been sleeping all that great. Oh well. There was always time to work on appearances later. As it was the Carters had already taken her in. Just the way she was. Justice looked towards the bed and realized how tired she felt. Maybe she would finally have a good night's sleep.

She walked to the bed a lay down. In minutes she was out.

The light knock on the door roused Justice from her sleep. Jane poked her head into the room. "Thought you might want a snack or something, since you weren't hungry for dinner. We're all having brownie sundaes down stairs if you would like to join us." Justice complied, and walked to the sit-down kitchen where everyone sat around the table eating sundaes. A spot was set for her and she saw that her own sundae remained waiting for her to claim. She sat down, and the family began to eat. After a short while Bill spoke, "Well how about we go around the table and tell a little about ourselves, huh?" Jane nodded enthusiastically, Vance just shrugged, and Valley looked like she might hit something.

"I think that's a great idea," Jane added, "I'll go first." She waited until everybody was looking at her and then continued, "Well, one of my hobbies is taking care of my garden outside. I just find it so relaxing to sit in the fresh air and plant my flowers. I love flowers, they are so beautiful. I also enjoy baking, and sewing. There that's a little about myself. Now Vance, why don't you tell a little about yourself?"

Vance announced that he liked most sports, and he was really into the new car that he had bought only last week. He loved hanging out with his friends, and really enjoyed going on hikes through the mountains.

Then it was Valley's turn. The little girl was stubborn, and refused to say anything other than she loved to sing, and dance.

Bill gave off a few details, and then suddenly Justice felt all four of the carter's stares on her.

"Well..." Justice began. She could tell them that going to the bar, and driving around drunk late at night was always refreshing, or that when she was sober she liked to head to the nearest gas station and pick up a few snacks, using the 5-finger-discount rule. However they may not like that in which case, she could always suggest that she liked going to the movies. That is, when she could slip away and see the latest, bloodiest film that was out. Out of all the things she could think of, she really didn't see the Carter's supporting any of her interests. Finally she settled on "Hanging out with my friends, and going shopping at the mall." Wasn't that what teenage girls were supposed to say? Normal ones, with normal lives anyway.

The family seemed content with that. The Carters talked around the table for a while longer. Justice mainly listened but would join in when asked questions.

Finally Justice retired to her room, and the thought that struck her seemed almost amusing, as she lay down to sleep. She hadn't even imagined sneaking out tonight. The thought hadn't even crossed her mind. "What do you know, miracles do happen." She mumbled as she pulled the covers over her head and sank into a peaceful slumber. Sleep like this didn't usually come so easy, but tonight Justice Clarks slept soundly.

Chapter Seven
Seeing the Other Side

Justice awoke to a beautiful morning. The sun was streaming in through the white curtains, and if she wasn't mistaken, the smell of pancakes seemed to hang in the air. Justice got up, made the bed, grabbed some clothes and headed for the shower. She massaged her head quickly with the sweet-smelling shampoo, and stepped out using a soft fluffy towel. She quickly slipped into her clothes and brushed her hair out. She decided to just leave it down and let it do it's thing. She would have time later to add a little bounce to the dead-straight locks. She walked into the kitchen and saw much to her delight (although she would never admit what an impact pancakes had on her,) a stack of them heaped up on a plate. It sat in the middle of the island, along with bacon, and eggs. Orange juice was already poured into glasses, and set around the table for each person. Jane looked up, a dripping spatula of pancake batter in her hand. "Good Morning Justice, how did you sleep?"

"Oh good morning," Justice replied." I slept pretty good." Did she *actually* say those words '*good morning*'? Man she was really starting to lose her touch.

"Well that is really good. How about some pancakes?"

Justice nodded.

Justice sat at the table and wondered where everybody else was. She knew that Bill was at the church, but since it was summer, she guessed that Vance was still around. She didn't really care where Valley was. The little girl was incredibly snotty. Vance came running down the stairs and into the kitchen.

"Mom, I'm gunna run out for a while okay?"

"Okay" Jane nodded, "But aren't you going to eat something?"

Vance threw a couple of pancakes onto a plate, and smothered it in syrup. He took about four forkfuls and gulped them down. It was like a race...how fast could he swallow. Just as quickly as he sat down he was back up and running out the door. He called back over his shoulder "thanks for breakfast mom, see ya Justice." Then Justice heard the door bang, and the garage door open. Valley came down then, rubbing her eyes, and whining about how much noise Vance had made.

Jane just smiled. So this was breakfast with the carters. Justice had seen worse.

Justice went back up to her room, and redid her hair. She noticed that the dark ends were starting to look a little split. Maybe a haircut would benefit her. She could probably cut her own hair. It wouldn't be too hard. Well, getting the back might take a little bit of practice, but she could do it.

"Hey girl," Jane smiled. Justice hadn't even heard her come in. "Checkin' out the split ends? If you want I can trim it up a bit later."

Justice didn't know what to say. She just nodded.

"Oh and I came up here to ask if you would like to go shopping for some new clothes."

"Love to, but can't."

"And why is that? Gotta be some where?" Jane questioned. Justice's reply caught her a little off guard.

"No, I don't have any money."

"Well I think I could take care of the cash part."

Justice couldn't believe what she was hearing. She really didn't get new clothes often. People would toss her hand-me-downs once in a while, but an actual shopping trip?

Jane must have seen the look on her face, and quickly said, "You see I've been wanting a shopping buddy for a while. I can't get Vance to go with me, and Valley complains the whole time. So here you are exactly what I need: a teenage girl."

"You don't have anything else planned for today do you?"

Justice quickly shook her head. As if she would have other plans. "No not at all."

"Great, than let's get going." Jane smiled and left the room to fetch her purse and keys.

Justice got her tiny black purse. It was a good thing she didn't have any money on her, it probably wouldn't fit in the little hand bag anyway.

Jane drove them to a mall a half hour away. She popped in a few good Christian CDs. Justice was surprised to find some of the songs actually had a pretty good beat to them. She had always imagined Christians listening to old hymns. The words weren't so bad either. Some of them she could even identify with. Jane made sure to keep the conversation rolling. Questions such as "Did she have a lot of friends?" "What kind of music did she like?" "What was her favorite subject in school?" "Did she have one?" Jane seemed to want to know everything about her, and strangely Justice wanted to tell her.

Jane finally pulled into a parking place, and hopped out of the car. "Now where should we go first?"

"I'm not really sure. I don't go shopping very often."

Jane wanted to hit herself. How insensitive of her? Obviously Justice didn't get to go out to the mall a lot. She couldn't fine a job anywhere. Susan had said it was because of her bad reputation. So why didn't Justice seem so bad?

They stepped inside the mall and the smell of hot pretzels and cinnamon roles filled the air.

"Hey I'm kind of hungry, what do you say we get a pretzel?"

"That sounds like a good idea." Justice smiled.

Was it Jane's imagination, or did Justice actually seem to be enjoying this?

They stepped up to the pretzel stand, and Jane ordered, "Can we have two salted pretzels?"

The cashier was a tall guy, with bleached-out blonde hair, and bright blue eyes, that Justice couldn't help admiring. She very *slyly* glanced at his name tag. It read *Wiley*. That wasn't such a bad name for him. She certainly couldn't judge names, Justice after all, wasn't the most common of them. She watched as he got their pretzels out of the little oven, and wrapped them up in white paper sheets. She realized that she was staring and tried to look away. Was it her head playing games or was he staring at her too? Everything seemed to slow down in the mall. *The noise died down to a slow hum, and the people prancing around with shopping bags, suddenly seemed to blur. His blue eyes seemed to hold her gaze without wavering and Justice could almost feel the warmth from his smile. He seemed to be speaking to her. Soft words. Although she couldn't be sure, she couldn't actually hear anything coming from his lips. Aw! His lips. They were full, and soft, especially for a guy. They were moving again, as he leaned closer to the counter...closer to her. She could see a smile twitching at the corner* of his lips, as he again tried to speak...the words seemed weird... 'Here', his mouth started to form, and then...something with a 'P'. Pretzel...Pretzel... Pretzel? PRETZEL!? Justice snapped out of whatever thing she was in. She wanted to swear.

"Uh, here's your uh, your uh pretzel." Wiley tried to hand it to her again, and this time Justice thankfully grabbed it and turned away quickly. She could feel the heat on her cheeks. How could she have been so OBVIOUS? He must have thought she was the dorkiest person alive! And she thought he was staring at her Ahhhhhh. The poor guy was only *trying* to pass her the pretzel she ordered. There she was thinking he was about to ask her some huge question like "Want to go out with me?" Man, and she was practically humming "Here comes the Bride" That was probably the furthest thing from his mind. Jane finished paying Wiley, and hurried to catch up with Justice, who had found a bench by the indoor water fountain. Wiley's face was a little red, but he only smiled and excepted her change. "I hope you ladies have a nice day." He had said. Jane had smiled, and muffled a laugh. Poor Justice. She sat next to the girl whose face was as red as a cherry, and put her arm around her. "So I guess you liked him huh?"

Justice only groaned. "Yeah. That was pretty much the worst thing ever."

Jane laughed. "He really didn't seem to mind your staring, you know. In fact, I think he found you attractive too."

Justice frowned, "He may have before, I acted like an idiot. Now I never want to see him again."

Jane had to stifle her laughter. She knew if she allowed one little chuckle she probably wouldn't stop.

"Okay so what do you say about this store?"
"I don't know. Do you think I could actually look good in

clothes like that?" Could she? That was funny.

"Well, there's only one way to find out."

So into the store they went.

Jane went through a clearance rack. "Hey this is kind of nice, don't you think?"

Justice looked at the light blue tank-top Jane was holding. "Yeah that's nice."

"I'm guessing that this color would look wonderful with your coloring."

Justice smiled at the compliment. They started out looking at shirts, but gradually made their way back to the jeans.

Justice picked out a pair of low hipsters, and Jane winced. "Hun, don't you think those are a bit low?"

"You think they are?"

"I don't think I would ever let my girls wear them."

"Girls?" Had she meant to say plural?

"Girl, uh Valley."

"Okay." Justice thought she might as well get what Jane wanted, since she was going to be paying for it all.

"Well what about these?" she asked, holding up a pair that weren't quite as low as the others.

"They look good to me." So they added it to their stack.

Justice made it to the fitting room, and found she liked most of what she picked out. A few pairs of jeans were to short on her and she had to exchange them for a longer size, but in the end she walked out of there with two new pairs of jeans, and the blue tank, that Jane had liked.

The pair went to another store, one that was much more upscale than any store Justice had ever been to. "Why are we going in here?" She couldn't help asking. She was never going to be anywhere nice enough for these sorts of clothes.

"You need some nice church clothes. I was hoping to find you a nice dress, or a few skirts, and tops."

Church? It really looked like they were going to try and take her along. "Well, you see Jane…" How could she put this nicely?

"I'm not a real big Jesus-freak." Justice winced, okay maybe she should have said "Church-goer" or "Sunday school –kinda gal." But no, in all her wisdom, and thanks, she said "Jesus freak."

Jane surprisingly laughed. "Well Hun, of course you aren't. Have you ever been to church before?"

Justice thought back. "I think one of my foster families took me to church once. I'm pretty sure it was for a Christmas service." The memory was pretty blurry because Justice was so young, and also because she had slept through most of it. It was mainly old Christmas songs, a crowed of old people, an organ, and little glowing candles dripping hot wax everywhere.

"Well then you really don't know much of what goes on in church do you?"

"Well…no."

"So then you should come and see for yourself. You can't rule something out unless you've already tried it…right?"

Well she did have a point. "I guess." She replied.

Forty-five minutes later, they emerged with a couple shopping bags full of dresses, skirts, and matching shirts. Plus, she got two pairs of high heels to go with them. Satisfied they walked into one more store, and bought a few more items.

Justice was beginning to feel hungry again, so they stopped at the food court.

While they munched on the subs they had bought, Jane asked Justice if she would still like to get her hair cut.

"Yeah just a few inches taken off, and maybe a little layered."

Jane smiled." Can do. I'm really glad you came with me today. I'm having a lot of fun."

Justice smiled." So am I. I can't believe you can't get your kids to come with you."" I know see, your just what I needed." Jane smiled. "I knew a teen girl couldn't withstand shopping." Jane almost looked sad as she said the last part.

" Are you okay?" Justice asked.

"Oh yeah." Jane looked up. "I'm fine…just trying to think of the best hair salon to go to."

But Justice knew that wasn't what she was really thinking. However, she had absolutely no idea what was bothering her.

They hit the hair salon, and Justice had her hair washed, cut and dried. Her shiny black hair gleamed in the sun-light as they walked across the parking lot to Jane's car. Justice realized what a great day she had. This had to be the first time any foster parent had actually wanted to go shopping with just her. She glanced at the many bags she was holding, and felt their reassuring grip. They were real, not just a dream. All of the bags filled with clothes just for her! Sometimes she had dreamed about having a mom to go shopping with. Most of the times she went shopping with her friends, and not even a third of the stuff they paid for…however they always seemed to come out with much more. She kept going along her daydreams, and became so completely absorbed that the dear girl didn't see the wonderful car pull right in front of her. Well actually, it swerved in front of her. Swerved not to *hit* her.

"Justice!" Jane screamed.

Justice looked up in time to see the car pull past her and slip into the parking space across from theirs. Thankfully the driver had been looking, otherwise Justice would have been flat. She had wandered far away in her daydreams, and also wandered into the middle of the road, as a car was coming by.

"Justice you scared me." Jane scolded her. "You have to watch where you're going."

"Yeah I know. I'm sorry I got a little lost in my head I guess."

Justice looked in time to see the driver of the car get out. His Bleached blonde hair and bright blue eyes were luckily turned away as she stared and thought for the second time, "Why me?" The guy had probably been out for his lunch break. He never expected to hit the same crazy girl who stared at him and acted like a loon.

She slipped into the car hurriedly, and hoped that she had escaped his notice…or at least not realize that she was the same girl who got lost in his eyes at the pretzel stand. That only made her groan more.

When they got home Justice took all of her new things to her bedroom, and began to hang things up. She put all of her church clothes together, and hung them in her closet, then folded her casual wear, and placed them in a drawer.

She slipped back down stairs after that, and nearly ran nose-to-nose with Vance, who happened to be running up the stairs.

"Whoa, sorry." He exclaimed, "I was just coming to find you. Valley said that somebody called for you."

"Oh, who called?"

"I don't know." Vance announced, "Ask Valley, I think she's in the kitchen."

So Justice went to the kitchen in search of Valley. She found her munching on a bag of chips, at the kitchen counter and asked as nicely as possible

"So did somebody call for me today?" Valley hopped off of her stool, and ran into the living room, where Jane sat on a couch reading. "Mommy, Some lady called for her." She pointed to Justice who came up behind her.

Well she could have just told me…why does she have to be such a brat? Justice couldn't help thinking.

"Thank you honey." Jane smiled at her daughter, "But next

time you get a call for Justice, tell her okay?"

Valley nodded, and then thrust the phone at Justice."

"Thanks." *You little brat.* Justice found that there was a message and realized that it was from Susan.

"Oh great, it's my favorite woman." Justice grumbled and walked outside, where she could talk privately. She dialed the number, that she knew by heart and Susan answered her cell phone on the second call. "Hello?"

"Yeah, is this gunna take long?"

"Yes I'm doing good, thank you for asking and how are you doing Justice?" Susan replied, in her very annoying way.

"I didn't ask, and I was actually having a good day, until you called."

"Well, you know how it goes. I call, and make sure you didn't actually run away, and that you are behaving yourself."

"So why don't you ask the foster parents you placed me with?"

"I wanted to hear your voice, and see if you were still there."

"Well now you know. I spent the night here, I'm getting along for once and so now I'm going to hang up." Justice smiled to herself. These were all the right things to make Susan think there really wasn't a problem, and hopefully discourage her from staying on the phone much longer.

"Uh Justice, I know that I can still take you to the mental hospital if you act up. So I'm warning you to behave."

"And I'm warning you that if you ever try to place me in one of those things, I will make sure you regret it."

" Justice don't threaten me like that."

"Then hang up the phone Susan and let me get on with my life."

"How are you liking the family?" Susan asked changing the subject.

"Like you care."

"Young lady, I really don't appreciate the way you talk to me. I'm doing my duty, and checking up on you."

Justice wanted to laugh. "Yeah I know, your just doing your job, looking after the little orphan. It's okay I know I'm just a job to you…something to make money from. So you don't have to waste your minutes asking how my life is. I know you really don't care. "

"Justice…"

"I'll do the honors." Justice hung up, and enjoyed the thought of Susan listening to a dead line.

What Justice didn't know, was that Jane had been listening in. Jane came up and placed a hand on Justice's shoulder.

"You know, I think you may have been a bit harsh with Susan."

Justice wasn't in a mood to argue, but she still bit out, "That's what happens when you have to deal with that woman for twelve years."

"I still think you could have at least been a little more polite. After all, she was just checking up on you."

"Yeah well, that's what she always does, but she never really cares how I like the home she places me in. She just wants me to be on my best behavior so I can live in a home forever, and she'll be done with me." Justice sighed, "So you see, it has nothing to do with me in the end. I'm just her job, and as long as I'm trouble, she has to keep spending her money to clean up my damages."

Jane nodded. "Well I can see how you would feel like that."

She was agreeing? The first adult to ever even *pretend* to understand.

"Come on let's go get dinner started."

"I don't know how to cook."

Jane raised her eyebrows and said, "Well then I guess you will just have to learn. We'll make spaghetti. It's not so hard to make."

They headed to the kitchen, "Valley you want to help Justice and me make spaghetti?"

The little girl nodded and said that she would like to help.

So Valley boiled the pasta, while Justice sliced tomatoes for the sauce. Jane was making garlic bread. They had a pretty good chain going, so dinner wouldn't take too long to make. The whole time Valley insisted on staying right next to her mom, and she pretty much ignored Justice. Justice wasn't so sure that Valley wasn't making faces at her behind her back. What did Valley have against her anyway? It wasn't like she had ever done anything to the girl. she barely said a word to her. Some girls these days…

The whole family sat down to pray at the dinner table.

"Dear Lord, we want to thank you for this food that you have blessed us with and we thank you for all of the many blessings that you give to this family each day. Thank you father, that Justice can come and stay with us, and we ask that we may all become better acquainted with her. In Jesus name, Amen." Bill finished the prayer and they all plunged into their meal.

Justice thought it was odd that he had mentioned her in his prayer. Sure she was staying with them and all, but he made it seem like a big deal to have her in the family. It was actually kind of nice. Jane told the family about their little shopping trip earlier that day, and announced that they had a wonderful time. Then she asked what Vance had been up to.

"Nothing much," He started in between bites of pasta, "I just hung out with some of the guys."

"And where did you go?" Jane asked.

"We went to the lake for a while, and then swung by a fast food place, and got a cheeseburger."

" Are these your youth group friends?" Bill asked.

"Yeah some of them."

"Oh and that reminds me!" Jane exclaimed excitedly. "Vance, you will have to take Justice to youth group tomorrow! I'm sure she will get along with some of the girls there." She smiled across at Justice. "The girls are really nice, I'm sure you'll make tons of friends."

Justice groaned inwardly. Jane had absolutely *no* idea what her friends were like. She had never hung out with any church-goers, and didn't really think she would have to much in common with them. "You know, I'm not so sure that we will have much in common. I'm not really used to youth groups."

Jane laughed, "Well remember what we talked about earlier? You have to try everything at least once. I think you'll be fine."

Justice Whished that she could be as confident.

The family talked on a little bit longer. Bill talked about the church and the new things that were going to start up soon. Valley remained quiet through most of the meal, except for the occasional "can you pass the water pitcher." Or, "The garlic bread please?"

After dinner, Valley raced up the steps and claimed the bathroom for her shower. Justice had been planning on taking one, but she guessed it was okay if Valley went first. At least the girl wouldn't be glaring at her for a while. Justice offered to clean the kitchen, and Jane exclaimed "Aw! How nice of you Justice! Now Vance, do you want to give her a hand?"

"Sure." He replied.

Vance gathered the empty plates that sat around the table. "I'll clear the table." He announced to Justice.

Not really sure where to begin, she answered that she would start unloading the dishwasher. The two of them worked for a while, and they both kept quiet. When Justice started cleaning out the pots, Vance offered to dry them.

"So how do you like the family so far?" He finally asked.

How did she answer that. "You guys seem nice."

"Nice huh?"

"Well what do you want me to say?" Justice couldn't help asking.

"Oh nothing I guess. So I hear you have kind of a reputation."

Was he trying to get her to reveal her bad side? "Yeah you could say that."

"So how did you build it up?" He asked as he wiped the remaining pot dry.

"Huh?"

"I mean," Vance said "What did you do that was so bad?"

Justice washed her hands in the sink and then carefully dried them before answering. "I've done a lot of things that most adults don't like."

"Oh I understand, but don't you make up with them eventually?" He asked trying to probe for more detail.

Justice sighed, slightly exasperated. Why did he care? "No, and if I'm lucky they throw me out the next day."

"Doesn't that make it hard to stay in a family for long?"

Now Justice was just plain annoyed, "Well duh, why do you think I've been in so many foster homes?"

Vance raised his hands in the air, "Hey just askin'."

"More like interrogating."

Vance laughed, "Man your rough to talk to."

Justice laughed back, "Well you don't shut up."

Vance was unperturbed by the comeback. "Hey, I just wanted to get to know my foster sis."

"Yeah well now you know." The kitchen cleaned, Justice walked up the stairs to her room, but not before she heard Vance call after her, "I can't wait to show you my youth group tomorrow."

"Yeah, what fun." She grunted. As she walked back to her room she passed Valley's. Was it her imagination, or was Valley talking to herself? Justice walked back to Valley's room, and listened to her. After a few moments she was pretty sure that Valley was talking to someone else. She kept out of sight and listened some more.

"Vanessa, this girl has to live with us now. She's really weird and I wish that she would just go away, and leave me alone. I try to ignore her, but mommy wants me to be nice to her. Mommy even said that she likes Justice, and that she wants to keep her for a while. She said that we will get to be good friends after a while, but I really don't think so."

Whose Vanessa? Justice wondered.

"You are my only best friend though, and I'm never gunna let Justice take your place, never ever. Even if Mommy, and everybody else does."

Justice raised an eyebrow. Man, yeah she had come into Valley's little family and invaded her life a little, but she wasn't out to take her best friend's place. No way. She didn't even want to be best friends with this brat. The things Valley had said about her didn't actually faze her too much, but she did wonder what Valley had against her. And just who was she talking to anyway? Justice peeked in just a little further. Valley was laying on her bed. And staring at the wall in front of her. She kept on talking, but as far as Justice could tell, no one else was in the room. How odd. Well she was a strange little girl, but then Justice herself was little different. She wasn't going to try and judge this girl.

She walked back to her room, closed the door, and got into bed.

Chapter Eight
The Real Meaning of Grace

It was Tuesday morning, only the second full day with the Carters. Still that was a big deal for Justice Clarks. As of yesterday, she was fully sober, and actually content. Breakfast had gone well, she had taken a shower no problem, and now she slipped into her brand new clothes. Her new Jeans and Light blue tank top, actually flattered her figure nicely. Justice decided to do something nicer with her hair today, maybe blow-dry it a little. She had seen one in the bathroom. It was probably Jane's.

Knowing that Jane wouldn't care if she used it or not, Justice picked it up and began drying her hair. The layers looked good, and gave her dead-straight hair a little bounce to it.

When she finished, she walked down stairs in search of Jane. Maybe she needed help with something. Justice found her in the living room curled up with the book that she had been reading the day before. "Good book?" Justice asked, as Jane looked up and smiled. "Yes, I've been enjoying it. You look beautiful in that outfit."

Justice blushed. "Thanks. You picked out the shirt."

" And it looks like I chose right. The layers are cute too."

"So what's your book about?" Justice asked taking the seat next to her.

"Well," Jane turned to face her. "It's Anne of Green Gables. It's about a red-headed orphan girl, who lives with a new family." Jane laughed. "Anne's not perfect you see, nobody is, but sometimes she does some really funny things. Anne also has a bit of a temper, and that gets her into a few rough situations."

Justice had to laugh. "Yeah you know, I think I could relate to her."

"Do you like to read?"

"Not a lot."

" Maybe you should read this when I'm done."

Justice looked at the book, and agreed that she would sometime.

"So what would you like to do today?" Jane asked her.

"Oh I was just hoping to explore the neighborhood a little, you know maybe take a walk."

"That sounds nice, you know you should get Vance to go with you."

"I don't know." Justice hesitated.

"Here, let me see where he is."

Jane walked to his room, and knocked on his door. "He's probably on the computer or something," she said, as Justice walked up beside her.

Jane heard Vance answer and opened the door. True to her word, Vance sat at his computer, dressed in shorts and a tee shirt. "Hey Vance, why don't you go on a walk with Justice. You know, show her the neighborhood and all?"

"Uh you know, I'm sure I can find my way around he doesn't have to come if he's busy." Justice stammered. She really didn't want to play twenty questions with him again. But Vance was curious, and so he agreed to go along.

"Just let me log off," he said, and quickly shut down the computer.

A few minutes later they were out walking in the sunshine, and enjoying the fresh air. It wasn't such a bad day. The sun wasn't too hot yet, and not a cloud hung in the air.

"So how did you sleep?" He asked her.

"Pretty good, and you?" Justice shot back.

"Not bad."

They stayed quiet for a few minutes, until Justice finally quipped, "Oh so you're done interrogating me huh?"

Vance just grinned, "Oh no, I still have a few more questions, but I was afraid that you might beat me up or something."

"What ever gave you that idea?" Justice raised an eyebrow.

"Oh I don't know, I just saw the tattoo on your shoulder, and thought maybe I shouldn't pick a fight with you."

Justice gasped and tried to look behind her. She should have remembered that. It was a rose tattoo, nothing evil or tacky, but still Justice couldn't imagine the Carter's liking it. Unfortunately, her tank top revealed the little rose. There was no question at all that Jane hadn't noticed it that morning when she had commented on her outfit. Yet she hadn't mentioned the tattoo at all.

"Don't get so freaked out, my family won't kick you out for a little rose."

"Yeah, but you would probably like that." Justice glared at him.

Vance laughed, as if the whole time, he had been trying to make her mad. Was he teasing her? She wasn't used to this annoying thing.

"Look, your probably just jealous because your parents wouldn't let you get one."

"Not that I would want one, but I could get one if I wanted."

"Oh what a rebel." Justice rolled her eyes.

"Hey, I don't want one because one day you'll get really old and wrinkly, and that little rose is gunna get longer and longer and more wrinkled, as your skin starts to stretch. Before you know it, your skin will barely be hanging on your bones. Then it will look disgusting."

Justice was trying to make her glare as cutting as possible, when she said, "Okay whatever. You never shut up do you?"

"Hey just trying to make conversation."

"And trying to drive me out of my mind."

"Hey what's a brother for?"

Justice swung a fist at him, but he simply ducked. "Aw that was cute." He smiled at her.

For once Justice didn't have much to say, so she walked faster. The houses in the neighborhood were nice, and although not huge, they looked well-cared for and most of them had pretty gardens in the front of the house, like Jane's garden.

"Hey wait up." Vance hurried after her. "You don't have to get all mad at me."

"Yeah well you are really, really annoying me."

"Sorry." Vance held back another laugh.

"Yeah, yeah. I'll give you a few more minutes, and you'll be back to your annoying self."

Vance hurried in front of her, and started walking backwards, still facing Justice as he said, "Hey I'll skip the minutes, and go back to my normal self now. So how long have you been in foster care for?"

"Since I was four." She replied without batting an eye.

"Man you must have been one rotten kindergartener."

Justice looked at him in disgust. "Uh huh, you should have seen me. All I did was behave, and share my toys. I was one of the most friendly, and one of the most talkative four-year-olds around."

"So what happened?" Vance slowed down, in hopes that she

would too. Justice did, but looked ahead as she replied,

"The families wouldn't want me, or they couldn't get all of the paperwork done on time. Some of the families I loved. " Justice paused. "I thought they loved me too."

"Wanna head back?" Vance asked her.

Justice smirked, "What are tired out already? Go ahead."

Vance not wanting Justice teasing him about being a wimp, decided to keep walking.

When they got home, Jane announced that Vance had missed a call from work.

"Did they need me to fill in for someone today?" He asked.

"Yes." Jane answered, "But I said that you couldn't make it today, that you already had other plans."

"What other plans?" He questioned immediately. He had been needing more cash, so as far as he was concerned, filling in for someone else was a good idea.

"Remember you have youth group tonight? You were going to introduce Justice to everyone there."

"Aw mom, we have youth group tomorrow too. I can take her then."

"Vance…"

"Please mom, I need the cash." Jane looked at her son. She sighed.

"Well I suppose I could bring her to youth group tonight. I could always introduce her to everyone."

Vance shot Justice a watch-out- for-mom look, and Justice stifled a grin. Jane was cool, but it might be a bit funny if she came to youth group, and introduced the 'new girl' around. Justice would feel like she was on a leash or something.

"You know what?" Justice piped in, "I think I'll just wait for Vance tomorrow. It's only a day away!"

Jane looked apologetically at Justice. "Are you sure? I know you were looking forward to meeting some new teenagers tonight."

"Oh yeah Jane, I'll be fine." She smiled her reassurance.

"Alright then."

Vance went to call his work back. "Sorry Justice!"

She couldn't have cared less. Phew, at least she got out of one visit with the 'youth group'. *If I can only make it through tomorrow...* She thought.

"Yeah she seems to be doing fine right now..." Susan paused. She was sitting at her office, and had the phone balanced on her shoulder, as she typed information on the computer. "Uh huh. She even stayed the night."

The voice on the other end spoke, and Susan answered, "Yeah, but there is something special about this family. Did you know that this is the first time Justice has had foster siblings? Yeah I know pretty strange. They just never trusted her with them before." Susan stopped typing so she could concentrate on what the person was saying. She held the phone snuggly against her ear. "Yes Justice is well aware of the situation. I told her and she really doesn't want to be brought in."

The line cackled, and Susan said, "Okay will do. Bye." She hung up and placed her head in her hands. The psychologist said that Justice should really be brought to his facility. He said the point Justice was at, was too much for another foster family to take care of. Justice needed to be at the mental home, under constant supervision. He also wanted to know about Justice's drugs and alcohol input. If she needed help with that too. Susan had announced that she wanted to try this one last family before sending her there. The psychologist hadn't liked that very much. However, Susan felt like she owed it to Justice. The girl had been through so much. Why not one last shot? Susan was painfully aware of all the things she had been forced to send to the hospital, in case they had to rush Justice in for an emergency break down. Susan had sent all of the files, and explained any extra little details. The Mental home now knew everything about Justice Clarks back round. Justice would flip if she ever found out. The girl never wanted to talk about her past, and didn't want anybody to know about it either. Susan remembered one time a few years back, when she was about to bring the file out to the foster parents awaiting to bring Justice home. Justice was about twelve years old at the time, and really didn't want the family to know anything about her past. She found the key to the file cabinet, and found her personal folder inside. It had everything from her birth records, to police reports about abusive parents. Justice took them out and burned them with a cigarette lighter. Susan went to fetch the files, and couldn't find them. On a slight hunch, she asked Justice if she knew where her file was. Susan never did find the ashes, but it didn't matter because Justice told on herself anyway. She had announced that she didn't want strange people poking around in her 'past' and so she burned them. Besides being on the verge of a break down, and fighting back the need to strangle the girl for doing such a stupid thing, she found herself relieved to have made photo copies of all the records only days earlier. She had them safe and sound in another box at home.

    Justice never knew about those. Thank goodness. Oh if only this new family worked out. Susan really wanted Justice to be happy, no matter what the teen might think.

It was getting late and Justice crept up the stairs to her room, she had been so absorbed in the book Jane had leant her, that she hadn't noticed the time. Midnight it was, and the lights were off in the house. All except one. Valley's light shown bright beyond the closed door. Justice leaned her head against it, and listened intently.

She could hear Valley talking to herself again…or to Vanessa? Whatever. She guessed all kids had an imaginary friend at some point in their lives. Wasn't Valley getting a little old for one though? Suddenly curiosity struck her hard, and Justice had to find out. She opened Valley's door slowly. Valley was laying on her bed staring at the ceiling, when Justice poked her head in she sat up and glared, "What do you want? Get out of my room!"

"Yikes, pipe down pip squeak, I just wanted to know who Vanessa is."

"None of your business! Get out!"

"Hey, I think having an invisible friend is cool! You know I use to have one too, but aren't you a little old…?"

"She's not make believe, and she's not a friend she's my sister!"

Justice was puzzled, "So she's real but nobody can see her, and she's an invisible sister, not an invisible friend?"

"No! I mean Yes! Get out now!" Valley yelled.

Justice was getting afraid that she was going to wake the whole house up. "Okay, okay. I was just curious okay? Why do you have so much against me? I didn't do anything to you." Justice backed out of the room with her hands held in front of her, palms up.

"You hate Vanessa, your trying to replace her!"

"No!" Justice laughed, "Vanessa's cool, huh we're friends right Vanessa?" Justice stared at the ceiling. "I won't take her place I promise."

That made Valley even more angry. She leapt off her bed, and onto Justice's back. Justice groaned "oof!" As Valley landed on her with a *thump!* Valley sunk her teeth into Justice's shoulder, and Justice shrieked with pain "Ahhhhhh! Get off you monster! "She finally managed to disengage Valley's teeth with her flesh, and flipped Valley over her shoulder and onto the bed. Valley leapt again with a cry of rage, but Justice was ready this time. Quickly she grabbed a pillow off the bed, and used that to block the attack. Valley fell back onto the bed and pouted. Justice took the opportunity, to leave the room and shut the door tightly behind her. "Sorry I bothered you!" She whispered safe behind the wood. She hoped she was. But with the power of the little girl's bite, she might just be able to bite through wood! Justice raced to her room, and turned the lock. She looked at her shoulder in the mirror, and saw the teeth marks. She winced. Hopefully Valley had all of her shots. She didn't want rabies or whatever it was you get from bites. Justice sat on her bed and looked out the window. The stars were twinkling, and the moon was out. Justice listened to the crickets sing. She liked how night could seem so still and quiet. Not to mention peaceful. She sat there for several moments. Finally she pulled the covers down on her bed, and turned out the lights. Justice lay there peacefully, slowly drifting off to dreamland. A thump on the window roused her, and she leapt out of bed. What was that? Justice longed to look out the window, but everything inside her told her not to. It was like some of the horror movies she watched…The actor in the movie would look out, and the audience would be yelling "Don't do it, don't do it!" Still the same thing always happened.

WHERE HOPE IS FOUND

The actor always let curiosity get the best of him. She leaned towards the window, and prepared to pull back the curtains... She was hoping that nothing would pop out, or that no hideous face awaited her... *Okay. One, two, three...* She yanked back the curtain, and shrieked!

"Ahhhhhh!" A face was pushed up against the window, and it could have been anything! Justice jumped away from the window, and grabbed a lamp off of her dresser, if the thing got inside, she could hit it with her weapon.

The face started to speak... "Justice it's just me, Janet. Could you open the window? I think I'm gunna fall."

Justice took a closer look. In the darkness Janet looked pretty creepy, what with her dark eyeliner, and heavy eye shadow.

"Oh my gosh! You scared me Janet!" Justice quickly opened the window, and let her in.

How did you know where I was? And how in the world did you get up here?"

Janet climbed in and shut the window. "Phew, that was a hard climb!" She stretched out her arms and then continued, "I heard Officer Anders talking about you, and I asked him if you had been placed in another foster home. He said that you had been taken in by a family at his church. Well, I found out what church he went to, and pretty much tracked down the family. I figured that you needed an escape, so here I am rescuing you."

Justice didn't know what to say. "Well, uh thanks."

"Yeah no prob, you can stay at my place. It turns out my roomie up and got married. She won't be back for a while. So yeah I'm kind of lonely, and not to mention stressed, because I have no idea how I'm gunna pay the rent now. Any chance you could pick up a job?"

"Well you know, I'm not so sure that's a good idea."

"What do you mean?" Janet demanded.

"I mean, "She paused. "Susan threatened to send me to some retarded mental home, if I don't get my act together. Not to be a party pooper or anything, but I *really* don't want to be there."

"Aw come on, are you going soft Justice? Susan's threatened you with a ton of things. She never enforces, and you never listen. What happened to your pattern?"

"I don't know. I really think she's serious about this one."

"Yeah whatever. Your just getting tamed. Man, I never thought I'd see the day that Justice Clarks got controlled by that lady."

Justice got defensive "Hey, it's not just Susan you know. It's this family. "She sighed. "They are actually kind of nice. They treat me just like the family, well except for Valley. She's a brat. My foster mom even took me to the mall, and bought me new clothes! Nobody's ever done that for me before." Justice watched Janet's face change, and she knew that Janet had never been on a mother/daughter shopping trip either. Her mom was a big time alcoholic, and never paid much attention to her. Janet grew up pretty much on her own. She never even knew who her father was.

"Yeah, well that doesn't sound so bad." Janet stayed quiet for a minute. "Well how about we go have a little fun at the bar? "

"No I don't think I can today. The Carter's wouldn't like it."

"So what? Your actually going to listen to them? Besides, the whole group's gunna be there."

"Janet, the group's always there. I doubt they ever leave."

Now Janet was getting a little annoyed, and she pulled the line that Justice was hoping she would say. "Well you know this family won't want you either. They will probably kick you out in a week or so. "

"Oh please. Don't try to encourage me." She exclaimed sarcastically. "The Carter's seem different. They'll keep me for a while, and at the very least, they buy me tons of stuff. I'm not going to throw away free stuff now am I?"

"Yeah well, I don't see anything different. Nice house, nice family, a ton of money. Wanna bet adoption is out of their budget? Face it. That's life. You'll always be Justice, the orphan."

Justice couldn't believe her ears. Was Janet really saying all of this stuff to her? "Whoa, what's wrong with you?"

" Oh come one. You've always said that about yourself."

It was true. She had, but for some reason the words didn't have that much impact when they came out of her own mouth.

Janet spoke again, "look I tracked you down, drove all the way her and climbed this darn window. Just to get you out. I thought we were best buds. I never expected you to put some foster family between us."

"I'm not, I'm just trying to lie low for a while, and you know gain a little more trust."

"Yeah whatever. Just come on Justice, I got stuff to tell you about Rick. Remember how we broke up? Well he wants to get back together now."

"Don't you dare get back together with that creep." Justice warned. "You deserve better."

"Well I'm considering it. If you really care about me you would come with me, and talk me out of it."

Justice rolled her eyes. "What if I get caught? Will you visit me in the mental home? I doubt it."

"Justice I would do that for you, but don't worry you won't get caught I'll make sure of it. I'll even drive you home afterwards."

"You better not drink." Justice sighed. "And is Officer Anders on duty tonight?"

"I won't, and no he's not."

"Okay. I'll limit myself to two hours, and I mean it…" Justice stared intently at Janet "I can't get caught."

"Done."

Justice, and Janet climbed back out the window, and Justice found that it was a hard climb. However, her long arms, and legs helped out a lot. Janet was tall too, and so she had no problem getting down.

Janet had parked a ways down the road so that she wouldn't wake anybody up, and cause a ruckus. So Janet and Justice walked to the car and hopped in.

Fifteen minutes later, they were parked. This was her home away from home. It was the place she always ran to, when hiding from another foster home. It was the place she first ran to, when she was twelve. Justice had never imagined being in another foster home after the one she had lived in for years, but she soon found herself tossed from home to home again. This bar had been her refuge for two days and nights. That's how she met Janet, and in time, the group that she still saw now.

As she walked through the doors, she spotted the familiar place. Everyone was there, and looking less than sober.

"Justice! Haven't seen you for days!" Greg slurred.

"You probably won't remember me for days either Greg, considering how drunk you are." She added.

Greg only laughed as if she had said something hilarious.

Janet sat down with the two beers she had ordered, and passed one to Justice.

"I thought you weren't going to drink." Justice scolded.

"Hey, only one I promise. Remember I have high tolerance?"

Justice wasn't so sure about that. "I really shouldn't be getting into this stuff now." She stared at the beer.

"Justice your back!" Ryan gave her a pat on the back. He had just noticed her walk in, so he slid across from her. "So what's the story this time? Where have you been?"

"I was at another foster home."

"So why did you ditch this one?" he questioned.

"Janet wanted to talk to me."

"So what was she rescuing you or something? How bad was this one?"

Justice tried to think of an answer that would please him. She racked her brain. Trying to buy herself more time, she took a sip from the beer Janet gave her. Almost without realizing what she was doing. What could she say about this one? Usually the insults about the families slid easily off her tongue in smooth, angry words. This time however, she was struggling.

"Well. The little girl seems to hate me, and acts all snotty around me." She glanced at Ryan. He didn't look too impressed.

"That's it?" He said as if he read her mind.

"No." Justice answered quickly, and took another sip of her beer. "They are this preacher family, and they have like all these rules and all."

"Like what?"

Justice was really starting to struggle. She took a big gulp of beer, and winced as it stung her throat. "Uh." She stammered.

Well she could tell him about Jane's kindness, or the shopping spree. Or if that wasn't bad enough, she could also add in that they made her really feel like part-of-the-family. *Oh no.* She thought. She was losing her reasons for sneaking out. Why had she done it again? Oh yeah, because Janet had needed her. Where was Janet anyway? Justice scanned the bar for her. Oh there she was with some guy in the corner. She was talking to him. Was that? Was it *really* who she thought it was? Rick.

Hadn't they talked it over the whole ride over here? Janet had finally agreed to never go near the creep again, much less get back together with him. So what was she doing with him now? Justice tried to see her face. She stood up from the table and glanced in that direction. Maybe Janet was laying it down for Rick. Telling him that they were over, and nothing was going to happen between them again. She strained her eyes, and let out a small gasp. Janet looked anything but mad. She actually looked like she was about to…kiss him! And so she did. Justice was furious with her.

"Hello, is anybody there?" Ryan snapped his fingers in her face. "What are you staring at?"

"Janet. She was the reason why I snuck out. I thought she said that she wasn't going to get back together with Rick."

Ryan looked puzzled. "Huh? Well I guess you wouldn't have known, seeing as you weren't here. They got back together two days ago."

Justice tried to keep the surprise out of her eyes. "Then she lied to me."

Ryan watched Justice's face fall. "Hey, maybe she didn't want to tell you, because she was afraid that you would talk her out of it. I know I tried."

"No you don't understand." Justice remarked. "I wasn't going to come at first, because I didn't want to upset the Carters…" her voice trailed off.

"Your foster folks?" He asked.

She nodded.

Justice sat back down. She stared at her beer. What now? So Janet lied to her. So what? They did it all the time. Justice could feel the anger and betrayal coursing through her. She got up from her seat, and slammed her drink on the table. Ryan actually jumped at her impulsiveness. "Hey what you doing?" He asked nervously. He watched her storm over to Janet. Ryan tried to call after her to just shake it off, but it was no use. When Justice was mad, there was no stopping her.

"Hey Janet." Justice called, well practically yelled at Janet's back. She was still making out with Rick, and was completely ignoring her. Justice groaned her disgust, and without another word, stepped in between them.

"Hey!" Rick protested. Jane only looked a little surprised. Justice glared at her and only then did she notice her blood-shot eyes, and silly grin. Janet had more than one beer that was for sure. Fighting down a new wave of anger, she started. "Hey I thought you were going to shake this creep." She turned her attention to Rick, he glowered at her.

"Whatya mean…" Janet slurred.

"We talked about it all the way here remember? That's the reason I snuck out!?" Janet looked surprised.

"You don't have to get so mad." Justice was even a little surprised at her own tone.

"No, oh come on. I just said something to get you to come. Look, I knew you weren't thinking clearly. I just had to tell you something so you would see the light." Janet had probably said more than she intended, but in her drunken state, she couldn't bite her tongue.

"You just *said* something? YOU JUST MADE SOMETHING UP!" Justice screamed so loud that everyone in the bar stopped and stared. Justice barely lowered her voice when she spoke next, "So your okay with the fact that maybe the one home I actually started to like…" her voice stopped. Justice could feel tears coming to her eyes. "I came here to help out my best friend. That's all. I never really wanted to go in the first place."

Janet nodded her head. "Okay well, here I'll take you home. She shot a quick look at Rick, who was sulking at a table. He left when Justice had screamed."

"… Just let me get my keys…" Janet said as she searched through her purse.

"Ah, don't bother. You're too drunk to drive, and I really

don't want to die with you. In fact I don't even want to be with you. So you can get back over there, with that abusive boyfriend of yours, and forget about me." Justice strode back over to her table, and chatter started back up in the bar. Some of the people in there had been expecting a brawl of some sorts. However, when Justice sunk back into her seat, they figured the excitement was over, and had gone back to their drinks.

"Hey, are you okay?" Ryan asked her.

Justice slapped her hands over her face, trying to smack away any stray tears that might fall.

"I—I don't know what I was thinking."

"Well hey you wanted to get away. I understand. Foster homes must be rough…"

"No." Justice cut him off. "They weren't so bad. They did all sorts of nice things for me, and really treated me like one of them." Ryan looked surprised.

"I've never heard you say that before." He gave a small laugh, then realizing that Justice wasn't laughing he stopped.

"Well I can always take you home if you want." He offered.

"To where? They won't take me back after this." With that she gulped down her remaining beer. She could already feel the alcohol numbing her system. If she had to mess up, then maybe this would ease the pain for a while. Ease the pain of losing another family.

Ryan was getting worried. When Justice got depressed, bad things started happening. "Come on let's go. I'll get the directions from Janet and then I'll take you back."

Justice cursed, "They won't take me back I messed up!" But Ryan found Janet and she luckily had directions scribbled on a piece of paper. She handed it to him, hardly realizing what she was giving him. There was no way that she would have been able to give him clearer directions, much less take Justice home. The girl was totally wasted.

Ryan returned to a tipsy Justice. She still seemed deep in her depression, and was actually starting to howl, as he half led, half dragged her out to his car.

"Aw come on, cut it out Justice."

"Just leave me here. They don't want me."

"You never know. They may never even have realized that you were gone."

"No, they'll know. They hate me, they all do. My mom, my dad, Susan, Jane, Bill, Valley..." The list went on and on. Ryan was feeling very uncomfortable. He had a feeling that Justice was saying more than she intended. He finally strapped her in a seat belt on the passenger side, and slammed the door.

He got in the driver's side, and started the car. "Just calm down Justice, I'll bring you home."

But Justice wouldn't have it. Almost the whole ride she whined, and cried, about things Ryan had never even heard her talk about. Things that she wouldn't be telling him if she were sober. Finally after a while, she settled down a little, and although did not fall asleep, she stayed still. Ryan turned some music on, and he felt a little more at ease. The street signs were hard to make out in the dark. It was about three in the morning, and there were hardly any cars on the road. He passed a little church, and then turned down the street. He found the house no problem after that, and wasted no time in pulling Justice out of the car. He made sure to park a little ways down the street, so as not to disturb the house with his headlights.

"Okay now be quiet. The lights are still off, so there's a good chance that they're still asleep, and haven't noticed that you've been gone."

Justice nodded. She seemed to lose her balance a little though and swaggered around. He led her up the porch, and set her down on the porch swing. "I'm going to leave you here alright?

Give me a call sometime and tell me how this all worked out." He whispered.

Before he headed back down the driveway, Justice whispered back. "Thanks a lot Ryan. You're a great friend."

Ryan smiled. "Hopefully all will go well with the Carters." He walked back down the street and got back into his car. Justice saw his lights turn on, and heard the engine start. Within seconds he was driving away. Justice got up then, and tried to get into the house. Luckily Bill had told her where they kept the spare key in case of an emergency, otherwise she would have been locked out without a way back in. And in the state that she was in, there was no way she could make it through the window.

At least she could figure that much out. Justice quickly fetched the key out of a potted plant on the porch, and inserted it into the lock. The door swung open, and she crept in as quietly as she could. Justice threw the key back into the pot, and closed the door gently. She locked the front door and headed up the stairs. Her legs weren't cooperation for some reason though, and she fell back down the few stairs she had already started to ascend. The sound of her tumbling down the stairs echoed through the house, and Justice immediately stopped and listened for any sign that she had woken somebody up. Nothing stirred so she tried again. But then she realized that she was thirsty. She tried to push the desire for water aside, but it kept coming back. Justice had to comply. She went to the kitchen and removed a glass. Holding on to the counter to help keep her steady, she went to the fridge, and got the pitcher of water out. In one hand she held the pitcher, and in the other she held the glass. Unfortunately, her vision was still a little messed up from the beer, and so when she tried to pour it, the water spilled everywhere, and the glass slipped from her hand. It fell with an ear-shattering crash to the ground. Bits of glass shot everywhere, and Justice slipped on all the water. As she fell the pitcher fell, and the remaining water spilled over everything else that had missed being drenched the first time…including Justice. When Justice fell she landed on pieces of shattered glass, and now she was trying to pull the little shards from her hands, and legs. Blood was starting to cover her hands, where cuts now replaced the glass that she pulled out. Since, Justice had never turned on the light, she couldn't see anything, and so she kept stepping on more broken glass, as she groped for the light switch. She let out a scream as she slipped on more water and fell again.

Suddenly the light turned on, and Justice could see. What she really hoped wouldn't happen, had just happened. Bill, Jane, and Vance had been awakened by the noise, and had come to check it out. Valley hadn't woken up.

Justice could only groan, and try to come up with some kind of excuse.

"Oh honey what happened?" Jane asked, as she stopped, and pulled Justice up.

"Whoa don't make another move Jane!" Bill warned. "There's glass everywhere!"

"Let me see your hands Justice! You have cuts all over them!" Jane looked scared, as she examined Justice's hands. "Bill these are kind of deep."

Bill quickly put on a pair of shoes, and then grabbed a broom. He rushed over and glanced at Justice's hands.

"Okay here, I'll sweep aside a path for you two to get across." Bill began to sweep, and Jane and Justice made their way to the bathroom. Justice was dripping blood everywhere. Justice couldn't seem to walk straight, so Jane guided her. Jane sat Justice down on the tub, and grabbed a wash rag from under the sink. After looking more closely, Jane realized that there were a lot of scrapes, but there didn't seem to be any glass stuck in the cuts. "Justice what happened? I thought I heard the front door shut, but I wasn't sure." Justice wouldn't meet her eyes. Or couldn't. She seemed almost out of it. Jane noticed how blood-shot her eyes were. "Justice have you been out…?" Jane started.

Vance ran in and asked, "Hey are you alright?"

Justice belched, and looked up sheepishly.

"Whoa," Vance coughed. "I think she's been drinking."

Jane second it, but with a quick shake of her head, Vance quieted. "Justice have you been out?"

Justice didn't respond.

"I expect an answer Justice."

Not wanting to disappoint them more, Justice nodded.

"Where did you go?" Bill came in then, and found the small bathroom crowded. "Why don't we move to the living room?" He suggested.

So off they went, Vance shaking his head, Bill wondering what he was going to do about everything, and Jane leading Justice to the couch. They all sat down and Jane repeated, "Justice Do you know what time it is? Where were you this late at night?"

Justice sighed, "I snuck out to the bar with my friends."

"This behavior is unacceptable in our house." Bill said looking at her disappointed. "You should know that."

Justice nodded. "I know. You can take me back to Susan tomorrow, I'll understand. "

"But…" Bill started.

"No, if you don't mind I'll go to sleep now, and then you can get Susan to deal with me."

"Justice that's not how we do things in this family."

"He's right." Jane agreed. "When we make a mistake, we sit down as a family and sort it out. Seeing as you are part of the family now, you will have to abide by the same rules."

Vance nodded.

"You mean your not throwing me out?" Justice looked shocked. "I get it all the time, no biggie…really."

Jane and Bill both shook their heads. "There really is no reason to throw you out. I'm sure if we did, you would just go to wherever you just were, and get even more drunk. Then you wouldn't have really learned anything from this, would you?" Jane announced.

Justice shook her head.

"No, we want you to follow the rules of this family. Just like everyone else."

Justice agreed. "Yeah."

"Now we are willing to give you another chance, if you can promise us that you won't do it again."

Justice thought it over. Saying she promised meant that she really wouldn't do it again. It wasn't just an escape route. It was a commitment. Did she really want to be stuck in this family forever? Did she really want to belong to Susan? "Yeah, I promise." She heard herself say.

"Good." Jane said. "Then I think we can finish up here. Are the band-aids still on?"

Justice nodded.

"Then I think we're all set. Bill got all the glass cleaned up."

"Thanks ." She murmured.

"Vance honey, you can go back to bed." Jane told him and led Justice up to her room. Justice collapsed on her bed, and Jane shut the door. As Bill and her walked back to their room, Bill spoke, "I knew we would have some problems."

"Yeah." Jane agreed. "But hopefully this will sink in, and she won't do it again. I think we have been very kind to her, trying to make her feel part of the family."

"We do have to think about it some. I mean if she doesn't learn from this and runs off again…"

Jane stopped walking, and looked at her husband. "Bill, she needs us. We have to help her overcome this."

"Your right, I'm just saying that she has never stopped running away before, why would she stop for us?"

"She came back didn't she?"

"Yeah, but that doesn't mean much."

"Bill, according to Susan, whenever she runs away it's because she's unhappy with the home she's at. She doesn't always come back on her own. Matt Anders always brings her back. You saw how sorry she looked." Jane protested.

"Yeah maybe sorry that she got caught." Bill looked towards Justice's door, "what's to stop her from doing it again?"

"Her word." Jane said.

"That doesn't mean that much."

"Then I guess we will just have to teach her that it does." Jane paused, and then said slowly, "Look, if she doesn't stop we might have to agree that another home would be better. We do have other children, and I don't want anything she does to rub off on them."

"Okay. Then we'll watch her, and make sure she's sincere."

"That and pray for her."

They looked at each other and nodded.

Chapter Nine
A New Crowd

Jane was in the kitchen making oatmeal when Vance came in. He looked troubled, and didn't seem to have slept well. None of them really had she guessed. "Good morning," she said to him.

Skipping the pleasantries Vance spoke what was on his mind. "Mom, it was my fault that Justice snuck out last night."

Jane looked puzzled. "How was it your fault?"

"If I had of taken her to youth group, she wouldn't have felt the need to get away."

Jane sighed. "Vance it wasn't your fault. Justice is responsible for her own actions. She did it, because that is one of her bad habits that she hasn't been able to shake yet."

"She does that a lot?" Vance asked.

"Oh yes. According to Susan. I talked to her the morning that we were going to pick Justice up. She told me some things about her, which she had failed to mention at first. Sneaking out late at night, and getting drunk was one of them."

"So she wasn't mad about not going?"

She laughed. "I think she could care less about going."

Vance agreed. "Yeah she didn't seem too thrilled to go."

"However, I would like you to take her tonight. She needs a

new crowed to hang out with."

"Yeah we'll definitely go tonight."

Jane scooped the oatmeal into a bowl and handed it to him. "Your older than her by a couple years. You can set the example. I can already tell that she looks up to you."

Now it was Vance's turn to laugh. "Yeah right. She treats me like an annoying younger sibling if anything."

"I think it's an act. She doesn't know what to say, so she hides behind her anger."

Vance sat down and began eating his oatmeal.

He got up and said that he was heading to work.

Justice eventually worked up the courage to walk down the steps. She had showered, changed, and even blow dried her hair. Something she hardly ever took time to do. Everything in the world to stall the very moment she would have to walk down the stairs, and face Jane. She knew that Bill had gone to the church for another meeting and wouldn't be back for a while, and she had heard Vance slam the door as he too, headed off to work. She had no idea where Valley was, but she had slept through the commotion anyway, so it didn't really matter to her. But Jane was probably cleaning the kitchen after breakfast. Justice was so afraid that they may have changed their minds, and were going to throw her out anyway.

She finally sucked in a breath, and headed down. Jane was right where she thought she would be, at the sink cleaning plates. "Good morning. I was wondering when you would come down."

Justice nodded sheepishly. "Yeah."

"Well do you have a headache after last night?"

Surprisingly she didn't. "No." Her only problem, was that she couldn't really remember much of what had happened. She could barely remember the conversation between her and the Carter's. The main thing she remembered was that they had agreed that she could stay if she promised not to sneak out again, and she had promised.

"Look, I'm sorry for last night." She apologized

"I know. Here, why don't you have some breakfast." Jane passed her a cereal bowl filled with oatmeal.

"Aren't you furious at me? Justice couldn't help asking. "Susan always yells, and takes my music away."

Jane laughed. "Is that how she punishes you? Well, I'm not much of a yeller, but I do get angry. Justice you did take away some of our trust in you, but we forgave you last night."

"Wow thanks." Justice said. She was shocked at her kindness. "But why would you?"

"Why would I what?"

"Why would you forgive me?"

"Because we all make mistakes. Justice when I make a mistake, I ask God's forgiveness first, but then I go and apologize to my family."

Justice nodded for her to go on.

"If Jesus can forgive me for all the bad things I've done, "Jane smiled. "Then I should be able to forgive you for sneaking out."

Why was she smiling? Justice couldn't figure it out. "Wow, that's really cool Jane. Thank you," she said. In all of her life she had never had an adult look at her like that, tell her she had done wrong, and then tell her that she forgave her. She never, ever had anyone smile after her sneaking out. Never. It actually turned out to be the complete opposite. Foster parents yelling, her breaking things and yelling back. Sometimes the police even got involved, and other times she was just locked out of the house until Susan came to pick her up. Nobody else believed in second chances. Most of them believed that foster kids would turn out to be trash, like most of their parents were before them. Jane, and the Carters seemed to be a one-of-a-kind family.

"Now, I do believe that you and Vance will be going to youth group tonight. They always have it two nights in a row. It's a different tradition, but we thought teens liked to spend more time together this day in age. It keeps them from going to other hangouts that aren't as…well, good."

"Yeah, I agree with that." Justice smiled.

"I guess you would know."

Switching the subject, Justice asked Jane, "So do you know about Valley's invisible friend? Or wait, I think it's her invisible sister."

Jane stopped everything that she was doing and focused on Justice. "You heard her talking to Vanessa huh?" Jane looked sad.

"Yeah, so I asked her about it, but she wouldn't tell me. She yelled at me too. Something about taking Vanessa's place."

"Oh no." Jane said, and put a hand to her forehead. "I was hoping this wouldn't happen."

"What wouldn't happen?"

Jane sighed. "I don't know how to tell you…"

Justice cut in, "Hey it's okay I understand. When I was her age I had an invisible friend too. I think it's just something that kids do when they get stressed out."

That didn't hit Jane so well. So Valley had similar problems to Justice? Great. "You're probably right." Was all she said. She didn't have the heart to tell her about Vanessa at the moment. She just wasn't strong enough. She had known that Valley had started talking to her, but when she had started telling Valley about Heaven, and how Vanessa loved it there… She thought Valley had stopped. Apparently it was still her coping method.

When Vance got home later that evening, he had it all planned out. The things his mother had told him earlier about Justice looking up to him, was really making an impact. He suddenly knew what he had to do. He had to talk to Justice about the rules in the family. If she knew that it was important, not just to his parents but to him as well, she might follow them more carefully. He had already told his mom and dad that he was going to take her to get a bite to eat with him and then go to youth group. They thought it was a great way for him to lay down the rules. Now all he had to do, was get Justice to come along. He knocked on her door. He heard a CD player on, and it seemed up really loud.

"Justice?" Still no answer. "JUSTICE!" He yelled. The music stopped, and the door opened.

"What?" She said, as she poked her head out.

" Hi." He replied. "That music was up really loud."

"Yeah, I like it that way." She looked down.

"Uh, so I was wondering if you wanted to get a bite to eat with me. Then we can go to youth group and I'll introduce you to all my friends."

"Okay…" Justice said, not seeming thrilled.

"My parents think it's a good way for us to bond, you know."

"Yeah right, okay I'll just get my purse." Vance walked back down the stairs and announced that she had agreed to go.

"Okay have fun." His parents said. He hardly thought he would.

Justice emerged, and they were off.

The car was awkward at first, and neither of them really knew what to say.

Finally Justice spoke, "I'm sorry about last night. I know I disappointed all of you."

Oh yeah that's what he was going to talk about. "I know. My

parents were really worried about you. That's why they got mad."

"Really? I must say they are the first."

"Well my family isn't like most families. Which is what I wanted to talk about." He paused.

"Go for it," she said, and so he went.

"Well you are a role model, did you know that?"

"Not really."

"Well you are, for valley that is. She's younger than you are, and she looks up to you."

Justice laughed. "She hates my guts. Good try though."

Vance had to smile. "Okay maybe right now she does, but she won't forever. She just takes a while to warm up, that's all. The point is that *one day* she will look up to you, and you can't be sneaking off, and yelling at people on the phone."

"You heard about my conversation with Susan huh?"

"I think the whole neighborhood heard."

Justice laughed. "Yeah, you just don't understand that women though. She makes me so mad."

"I know what it's like to hate the social workers."

Justice tried hard to keep the anger out of her voice as she snapped, "Uh, no offense, but you don't."

Vance kept driving letting the comment slide. He pulled into the parking lot of a fast food restaurant, and leaned back.

Justice kept still not sure what he was about to say. Maybe get out?

"Actually I do. I was adopted too Justice."

Justice was shocked. "What!?" She stammered, "I thought you were just part of their family, you have the same coloring and all…"

"Yeah, most people never know I was adopted, but I was."

"How old were you?" Justice asked.

"I was nine." So he wasn't exactly born into their family.

"Wow. I never would have known. You're so…calm. For a…you know…"

"For being adopted? Well, I had my problems too. My sister helped me though."

"Your sister? Valley would have only been a baby, how did she help…?"

"Not that one." He cut in. "My other sister. She was two years younger than me. Three years ago, she died. She taught me how to fit in with the family."

Things were starting to make sense. "Was her name Vanessa?"

"Yeah. How did you know?"

"I heard Valley talking. She said her sister's name was Vanessa. I thought it was like some kind of invisible friend." Justice closed her eyes at the thought. She had said a lot things last night. She had gone in trying to get closer to Valley. That conversation probably pushed them further apart.

"Yeah, she likes to pretend that Vanessa's still around. She's been a lot better. She use to insist that she was still alive, and would often set the table with Vanessa's spot included. She definitely took it the worst. Valley was really close with her. We all were." Vance looked away sadly.

"I'm sorry." Justice offered. She really knew what it was like to miss someone you loved. It was heartbreaking.

"Anyway, she was there for me when I was angry at the world, and now I'm going to be there for you. "

Justice looked at him surprised. "What do you mean?"

"We are going to control your temper, and get you hooked up with the youth group."

She groaned.

"It's really not that bad. You'll see. Now, let's go in and order. I'm starved."

Justice was feeling overwhelmed. Suddenly Vance had told her the family's deepest pain. Now she knew about it. Why Valley hated her so much, and how Jane looked sad sometimes. Why the whole family was so strong. They had been through something that was at least equal to her own pain. Maybe that's why she was finding it easier to stay with this family. Now Vance was telling her that he was adopted at the age of nine. Wow a lot in common already.

They ordered their food, and sat down at a table with it. Vance ordered a cheeseburger, so Justice went with the same. He dove right into his, but she was dying to know more. "So were you in foster care for long?"

He looked at her over the huge burger. "For four years."

"Not that bad."

"It felt longer. The social worker who dealt with me was much worse. He was always pretty mean. He would place me with just about any family. Sometimes the families were mean, and would single me out from their own kids. I was only five, and really scared after my parents deaths."

"If you don't mind me asking, what happened?"

"My parents died in a car crash and I didn't have any other relatives. My life was great until the day they died."

"That must have been awful."

"Yeah it was. I was a different kid after that. I guess the four years of foster care pretty much destroyed any decency my parents had taught me."

"Yeah, well at least you had some."

"What about that one family you were talking about?"

Justice stiffened. "I don't know what you're talking about."

But Vance could read it in her face. "Come on, if you don't want to talk about it just say so. I've been open with you, so you should be open with me."

"Okay fine." She took a big bite of her cheeseburger, just to give herself more time. She could feel a lump rising in her throat. There was no way she was going to cry. Not here, and not now. Especially not in front of Vance.

Vance rolled his eyes, as he watched her chew and chew. "Alright fine. I guess it's to painful to tell me about. It's okay I really don't want you to cry about it either."

Whoa, that remark made her mad. She had to say it now, just to prove that she could. "They died in a car accident too, when I was twelve. I was placed back in foster care after that. From then on, Susan was making my family arrangements. She pretty much sucked at it too."

"Okay, now we're getting somewhere."

"What is this, a therapy session?"

"Maybe."

"Yeah well many psychologists have tried to change me, and everyone of them fails."

"I'm not trying to change you, I just want you to find a better release for your anger. Drugs and Alcohol don't numb it forever."

Grrrr. He was setting her up. Trying to make her trip, or spill things just to get her in trouble. "Who said anything about drugs?"

"Well I only assumed..."

"Okay fine, whatever. Think the worst about me."

Vance shot back, "Well you won't tell me about you, so how am I supposed to know differently?"

Justice did see his point, but really hated to admit it. "Okay I'll tell you a little more about me. What do you want to know?"

"Hmmm... I'll let you know when I have more questions."

Justice growled, "Yeah I'm sure you will."

"Okay, are you almost done? I don't want us to be late for Youth Group."

Justice got up and threw her empty wrapper away. "Yeah, but are you sure you don't want to go somewhere else?"

Vance got in the car, and although he knew better, he couldn't help asking, "Like where, the bar?"

She jumped in too, and reached over to hit him. Well actually it turned into a punch, and it landed on his shoulder. It was pretty hard for a girl. "Ow." He remarked as he started the car. "That was pretty hard. "

Justice had expected a bigger reaction from him, but he merely shrugged it off. Vance pulled out of the parking lot, and pulled onto the road. "I'm just not so sure that I want to meet all of those…church people."

Vance shrugged, "Well find out. I'll introduce you to everyone. "

Justice wanted to argue more about it, but found it would probably be useless. The whole family wanted her to go.

They walked up to the church, and Justice could feel her insides flipping around. She felt a little shaky, and really out of place. Why was she so scared to meet new people? She did it all the time. Maybe it was just because these were really religious people, and she wasn't really use to this crowed. She followed Vance inside, and looked around, ready to run out the door if anything unexpected happened. They seemed to have walked into a big room. There was a TV in one corner, and a table on the far side of the room. It was covered with chips, and soda. Loud music was playing. She recognized one of the songs that she had listened to in Jane's car. The music was heavy, almost the same kind she liked, except a lot cleaner. There were a ton of teens in the room. Vance explained that the ages ranged from thirteen to nineteen. People were laughing, and joking around. Some girls were dancing to the song, and guys were trying to follow the dance steps. Everyone in the room seemed to know how to act around everyone else. They were all friends, and nobody looked like they had a hangover.

Vance told her to follow him. He led her to a group of teen's two girls and a guy. "Hey everybody, this is my foster sis, Justice." The two girls spun around. "Hi!" One said. She had blonde curly hair, and cute glasses that you could barely see. "My name's Emily." The other girl stuck out her hand. She was Black, and had straight black hair that hung to her shoulders. She wore a big smile as she introduced herself as Tanika. The guy spun around, and Justice thought her heart stopped beating. She wanted to hide behind Vance. His Bleached-out blonde hair should have tipped her off, but she was to busy being introduced to Emily, and Tanika to get away. What could she do? Before further escape plans were given, Wiley extended his hand and said "Hi I'm Wiley."

"I'm Justice."

"Nice to meet you Justice." He smiled and Justice thought she was going to drop dead. Did he remember her? Oh please don't remember her! She searched his eyes for recognition. If he did recognize her he hid it well.

Vance stepped in, and slapped Wiley's hand, "Hey, I'm glad you made it tonight, you haven't been here in weeks!"

"Yeah I know." Wiley said.

"Still into taking pictures?" Vance teased. He explained to Justice that Wiley had decided to be a photographer and now photographed every flower and tree there was.

"Yeah, well I've been really busy with that, and work."

"The pretzel stand get pretty busy?" Vance teased again.

Wiley smiled. He looked over towards Justice, and she swore he remembered her. "Yeah it's been pretty busy."

"So how long has Justice been with you guys?" He asked.

Vance looked at Justice. Her face was a little redder than usual. She must have been a little overwhelmed. "A couple days."

"So how do you like the Carters?" He asked her.

Justice laughed. "They're pretty cool I guess. Except for Vance." He gave her a playful swat on the arm.

Wiley laughed. Wow she had made Wiley laugh! Her heart jumped, but she stopped herself before she went off into dream land again. That's all she would need. A relapse of last time. Yikes.

A guy who must have been in his mid-thirties came into the middle of the room, and asked if everybody would take a seat. Chairs were pulled from various corners around the room. Everybody sat down. Justice took a seat next to Vance, and Wiley sat next to her. She tried to conceal the excitement that out of *all* the girls in the room, he had chosen to sit next to her. She looked around. Okay, so maybe there weren't any other chairs in the room, but he could have chosen to sit on the floor right?

The guy in the front of the room noticed Justice and asked, who Vance had brought with him. It reminded Justice of show-and-tell in first grade. He then introduced himself as Mike, the youth pastor. Justice smiled, and said a hello back. A lot of the teens in the room were staring at her, so Mike asked everyone to share their names, so they could get to know her, and she could get to know them. After they went down the rows and said their names, Mike asked if anyone would like to pray. Vance offered, and they all bowed their heads. Justice did the same. Did she bow her head like this? Was she supposed to close her eyes? She looked over at Vance. His eyes were closed. She quickly closed hers. Then she remembered it was just like what they did before they ate at the Carter's house. Only Vance wasn't thanking God for his food, he was asking him to be with them tonight, and guide them through their study. What study? Justice was confused. How would God guide them?

Vance said an 'Amen'. And they all opened their eyes. Justice quickly lifted her head and looked around. Everyone else had lifted their heads too. So far so good. She was fitting in. Then Mike asked if some people would like to lead them in worship. A few teens walked up and strapped on guitars, and raised up microphones. One kid got behind a drum set, and began to thump a beat, then the guitar joined in, as well as the keyboard. Pretty soon the singers started singing. The songs were fast and filled with Praises to God. She watched as some teens lifted up their hands, or danced along, while other stood still with their eyes closed. It didn't seem to matter what they were doing...they all had the same look on their face. They were all praising their Lord. There was a difference here, Justice realized. She felt a peace, and something much more in this room, with these people. It was something that she had only felt in the Carter's home. She never really knew what it was, but something inside of her longed for more. After the singing stopped and all of the instruments put down, or turned off, Mike came back up to the middle of the room and preached. Justice had never really listened to a sermon before. She had always imagined them as long boring, speeches that dragged on forever. This one only lasted for about fifteen minutes and it wasn't all that boring. She would never admit it though. After that was done, they sang another song, and then the group was open to discussion about the sermon or free to go to the refreshment table. Everyone started to chat eagerly. Many girls came up and introduced themselves to Justice. She tried to be polite and introduce herself, but she was feeling pretty overwhelmed.

"Want a soda?" A voice asked behind her. She spun around and saw Wiley offering her a can of Pepsi.

"Uh sure, thanks."

"It's a pretty big group huh?" Wiley asked smiling.

"Yeah it sure is." Justice raised her eyebrows. "I'm still trying to memorize everybody's names."

"Yeah, don't worry you'll figure them out soon."

Vance came up then, and asked her how she liked it. "It's not as bad as I thought it would be." Justice whispered to him.

Everybody turned out to be pretty nice, and she didn't feel like she stuck out as much as she thought she would. The people here didn't seem that judgmental either. She never saw anybody left out and alone the whole time. The youth pastor walked up to Justice and shook her hand. "So glad to have you here Justice." He smiled. "Pastor Bill, said that you would be staying with them. Are you settling in pretty well?"

Pastor Bill. She had almost forgotten. "Yeah the Carter's are pretty nice."

"Yes they are."

Vance tapped her on the shoulder again.

"Well, I'll let you meet some more people, I just wanted to come over here and introduce myself." Mike smiled.

"Nice meeting you." Justice smiled back.

"Hey Justice, Wiley and I are going to the movies tomorrow, do you want to come?" Vance asked.

Justice wanted to whoop for joy. If Wiley was going, so was she! "Ummm..." She pretended to think. Couldn't seem anxious or anything. "Yeah sure, sounds fun."

"Great." Vance said. "Oh yeah, and I asked Emily and Tanika to come too."

"Okay." Justice said. So two other girls were coming too...no big deal.

"Well we better get going. See ya tomorrow guys!" Vance waved, and so did Justice.

"Nice meeting you!" Wiley called after her. Tanika, and Emily waved.

Vance got in the car, and waited for Justice to shut the door, before he asked how she thought it went.

Justice reluctantly admitted that it wasn't as bad as she thought it would be at first.

"And you made new friends out of the whole thing right?" Vance prodded.

"Yeah, yeah, yeah. I made more friends are we good now?" Vance gave her a big cheesy grin.

"I'm so proud of you." He gushed.

"Aw cut it out Vance."

"Okay, okay," he said growing more serious. "So are Christians like aliens from Mars, or are we not so bad after all?"

Justice thought about all the people there. She didn't hear any swearing, or smell any alcohol. There was no punching and shoving, and everyone seemed to respect everybody else. Over all the teens were pretty nice, decent people. She would never consider Wiley as a weird alien. "No, you guys are alright I guess."

Vance smiled, and focused on the drive home. When they got through the door Bill walked into the living room to greet them

"How did it go guys?" He asked.

"Pretty good." Vance answered.

"Good."

Justice sat down on the couch and laid her head back.

"So what did you think of Wiley?? Vance teased.

Ahhhhhh he can't know! "He seems nice. You guys been friends long?"

"Oh come on. I know you like him."

"Oh Vance would you shut up?" Justice tried to glare at him, but her cheeks were starting to blush, and she was trying not to laugh.

"Sure, but are you excited about going to the movies tomorrow?" He cleared his throat. "I happen to know he's coming with us."

That was it, Justice grabbed up a pillow from the couch and smacked him with it. He ducked though. He was pretty good at dodging things. Justice guessed he had to be, for the amount of teasing he dished out.

He snatched a pillow from the other side of the couch and swung back. He caught Justice on the side of the head, and her hair flew in her face. Vance laughed.

"Wow I guess you do like him."

"Vance, I never said I liked Wiley!"

"Now that name sounds familiar." Jane said coming into the living room to see what the commotion was all about. "But where did I hear it?" She winked at Justice.

"Whatever. Well I think I'll go to bed now." Justice said, trying to get out of the trap they had set up. Jane laughed. "Good job, you got out of it this time, but next time you won't get away so easy." Justice knew her face was blushing bright red, so the sooner she got upstairs the better she would feel. She automatically stopped by Valley's door on the way up. She heard the girl talking again. She couldn't help feeling a little sorry for her, and she tried really hard to not feel anything for anybody other than herself. Maybe one day Valley would want to tell her about Vanessa. She walked into her room, changed into a baggy tee shirt. Justice checked the window to make sure it was locked. No more temptations for her. She almost got herself kicked out of another foster home. She was really surprised that the Carter's hadn't even called Susan to let her know about last night. She got under her covers, and began to day-dream about the next day…

She was sitting in a corner all by herself, her hands clasped tightly around her little head. The yelling and screaming was getting out of control. She knew that in a moment they would start hitting each other. If she stayed here, than maybe they wouldn't hit her. Her little belly growled, and she wondered when she would finally be allowed to eat again. Her mother hadn't been to the grocery store in over a month, and the little girl had been living off of stale bread, and old food she found lying in the dirty pantry. Her mother never ate these days, she always went out at night, and didn't come back home until the next night. The little girl was often forgotten about, and she spent many nights on her own. They screamed awful things at each other, and just as she had thought, they started hitting each other. Her mom's lips, and nose were bleeding, and she was screaming. The little girl didn't know what to do. She didn't like her mother screaming, but yet she didn't want to get to close. Her dad stormed out of the dirty little house, and left his wife a helpless mess. He hadn't looked so great either. His nose was bleeding too, and he had big scratch marks across his face. In a moment the little girl could hear tire screeches as her dad pulled out of the driveway. She could only imagine how long he would be gone this time. Last time he had been gone for months. Her mother was sobbing on the floor, and was holding her head in her hands. The screaming had stopped, but the sobs that can only come from a truly broken person filled the shabby little house. The girl tried to tip-toe around the sobbing mother. The lady picked her head up and swore at her daughter. The little girl tried to run, but the lady grabbed her, and tackled her to the floor. "This is all your fault!" The lady screamed.

"I'm sorry, I'm sorry!" The little girl screamed, as she tried to shield herself from her mother's blows. The lady slapped, her again, and again, until the little girl thought she couldn't hold on. She opened one eye, and saw a giant fist...She screamed.

"...Ahhhhhh!" Justice screamed, sitting straight up in bed. She was drenched with sweat. Her hair was matted to her face, and she found that she was trembling. "Just another nightmare." She mumbled. She couldn't slow her breathing though. The dream was to vivid, to painful to let go. She glanced at the clock. It was four-in-the-morning and she hoped she hadn't woken anybody up with her screaming. Sometimes she had these nightmares. This was the first one that she had since she came to the Carter's up. The last one she had, was the night she snuck out of Mr. Allen's house. It was what had caused her to sneak out and hit the bar that night. She had never mentioned them to anybody, but on some of the nights she had to spend with Susan in the office, she had them. Susan had woken her up a few times, and asked if she wanted to talk about the nightmare. Justice would always reply angrily, that she was fine, and no, she didn't want to talk about her 'dream'. Which is what she always called them. She never wanted anybody to know about them. It would show weakness she feared. Weakness was not something she wanted anyone to think she had. Weakness was what got people hurt in this world. Showing fear of a nightmare was weakness. So Justice closed her eyes and tried to go back to sleep.

On Wednesday evening Justice was all set to go to the movies with Vance and his friends. She had taken extra special care to make sure that she looked nice, this morning. Not that she was trying to impress anybody. Nope that certainly wasn't it. Jane asked if she would like to borrow some eye shadow to match the shirt that she had on. Justice had at first said no, but then thinking it over she let Jane give her a little make over. It was actually kind of fun. They were all ready to go, and so Vance started the car and off they went.

"So when are you going to learn to drive?" He asked her.

"When someone will trust me enough to take me." Justice scowled. "For some reason I can't get anybody take me to driver's

Ed, or get my permit. Nobody wants me behind the wheel."

Vance laughed, and thought that was hilarious. "I guess they think you'll turn out to be an aggressive driver."

"Yeah that's probably exactly what they think." Justice chuckled. "So what movie are we seeing?"

"No clue, I guess we'll decide when we meet up with everybody else." Vance turned on the radio, and they listened to that the rest of the way.

Justice hopped out of the car and started to the theater with Vance. The whole group awaited them inside, and they met up and talked casually. Justice mingled a little bit, but was keeping one eye on Wiley the whole time. He looked nice today. She smiled. He was laughing and talking to Vance. She had no idea what he was saying, but she loved the way he laughed.

"So what kind of movies do you like?" Emily interrupted her daydreams, which was probably a good thing, seeing how that seemed to be happening a lot lately. "Uh, all sorts. What about you?" Justice realized that she hadn't really answered her question directly, but she really didn't want to tell her all of the ones she liked.

"Well," Emily started. "I like Action, comedy, and of course every girl loves a good chick-flick." She smiled, and laughed.

"Yeah that's true." Tanika agreed.

They finally decided on a movie and all five of them got in line to buy a ticket. Justice was waiting in line for her ticket when she felt a tap on her shoulder. She spun around and groaned. "Hi Officer Anders."

"Hello." He replied cheerfully. "So I see you survived Susan. After the look on her face when I brought you back last time, I really thought I may never see you again."

Justice laughed, "Yeah I really ticked her off that night."

"So, your still with the Carter's right? I mean your not here alone are you?"

Justice laughed again, "No, actually I'm allowed to be out for once. I'm here with Vance and his friends."

Vance spun around at the mention of his name. He had just paid for his ticket, and so he dropped back and said hello to Officer Anders.

"Wow you are actually with someone this time." He smiled.

Vance laughed and said "Why she out here a lot?"

The cop smiled. "Yeah I find her sometimes."

"Well we should get going Vance, the movie's starting soon." Justice announced, anxious to get away.

"See you later Justice."

"Bye!" She replied, and walked away quickly.

Vance shrugged, gave a wave of goodbye, and followed Justice into the theater.

The movie wasn't terrific but they all had fun, so it was worth it. They came out of the theater laughing and talking.

Wiley leaned over and asked Justice how she liked the corny film.

"It was okay. I thought it was funny, in a cheesy sort of way."

"Yeah it was." Wiley agreed and laughed again.

"So do you go to the movies a lot with your friends?" He asked.

Justice shrugged. "Sometimes. My friends aren't really into that sort of stuff."

He asked the inevitable, "So what are they into?"

Justice looked at him, trying to judge his reaction. "They're kind of party people. They like to sneak out and go to bars, or big wild parties."

Wiley nodded, as if he knew what she was talking about. "Yeah, I use to have friends like that." He paused. "Until I met these guys. I suddenly realized that the people I was hanging out with, weren't really the people I wanted to be with anymore."

Justice was surprised." So you just quit hanging around with them?"

Wiley shrugged, "Pretty much."

"But what happened when you saw them around? Did they ever ask you questions, or guilt you into coming back to their little group?"

"Sometimes, but I just explained that I didn't agree with everything that they were doing and well, that I had changed. I wasn't into that stuff any more. It was over. As soon as I established that they left me alone. Of course we never hung out again, but it was all good. I had a new group of friends and a big church that could become my 'new group'."

"Man, I wish my friends were that understanding." Justice muttered without even realizing it. When she did her eyes got wide.

"Are you trying to break free of a group Justice?" Wiley asked her. Justice studied him. He seemed understanding enough. Maybe she could tell him some of her thoughts.

"Well, I guess you might say that." She sighed. "Okay, the other night I snuck out. I've done that a lot in my life, but the other day I felt really bad about it. You know what I mean? The Carters were so nice to me, and yet I snuck out and betrayed their trust. I did feel sort of bad about it. Is this making sense?"

He nodded that it did.

"Well, the only reason I agreed to sneak out was because my friend needed help making this decision..." Justice went on and told him the whole story. "...Anyway, I couldn't believe my best friend would do that...she just really didn't get how much she could have messed up my life with that one simple lie. I know it was my fault for going, but it still didn't seem right..." Her voice trailed off. "I don't know. Maybe I should have known."

Wiley thought a moment and then said, "Well maybe she's not a true friend. Well, okay a *real* friend wouldn't have pressured you into going. Your right, I don't think she had a clue about how much damage she could have done. If a friend is that clueless…well you really do have to ask yourself, if she is really your friend."

"Yeah." Justice agreed. "I guess, but I really don't know what to do about it. "

Wiley smiled, and Justice felt her heart beat faster, "Well hang out with us then. You can worry about them later."

Justice nodded. Wiley looked at his watch. "Ah, I guess I better go. I have a pretzel stand to run. Nice talking you Justice, we'll all have to meet up again soon. Maybe Saturday…? Hey guys want to do something Saturday?"

Emily said that she couldn't because she was going away on vacation for a week, but Tanika, and Vance agreed. So it was set.

"Great, well I'll see you later!" Wiley gave Justice a friendly hug and shook hands with Vance, before he raced off to his car – the same one that had almost smashed Justice just days earlier. They said good bye to Tanika, and Emily, and headed towards Vance's car. When the doors were shut Vance let out a whoop and started an annoying song/chant of "Justice got a hug from Wiley, Justice got a hug from Wiley!" Thoroughly embaressed, Justice turned on the radio to drown out His annoying ravings.

Dinner was nice that night, with the whole Carter family talking about their day. When it was Justice's turn to speak, she announced that she had a good time at the movies, and the whole family erupted in laughter. Apparently Vance had spread news about the little hug. Good ol' Vance. Justice didn't really mind the teasing so much now. She hadn't played around like this for years. She decided to try and dish out a few jabs of her own. "Well you know, you sure talk to Emily a lot Vance." She winked, and he actually blushed. That made the family laugh again, and Valley began to sing a little song of her own, about Vance and Emily sitting in a tree.... After dinner, Justice was doing the dishes, when the phone rang.

"Would you mind getting that Justice?" Bill called from the other room. He was busy e-mailing a church member in the other room.

"Sure." She replied. And grabbed up the phone. "Hello?"

"Hi...is this Justice?"

Justice recognized the voice anywhere. "Hi Susan."

"Wow I actually got a hello from you!"

"Thrill of thrills." Justice smirked.

"Well, so how is everything? Oh wait, I'm not supposed to ask that...um, well have you been a lot of trouble?"

Justice thought about her incident. Well there was no way she was going to tell Susan about it if she didn't have to.

"I hung out with people at their church today," she said, knowing that Susan would be surprised.

"You did? Wow, I must say I'm impressed. But were you handcuffed to them, and dragged along? Or did you actually go on your own free will?"

"Really Susan, this is what gets on my nerves. I actually went along. See? I'm no problem, now I'll talk to you later."

"Okay, you know what I have to go too, I just wanted to make sure things were still running smoothly. I'll talk to you later too."

"Great look forward to it. Good bye now." Justice hung up quickly.

Jane came into the room, hand over her mouth to cover a smile. "Well, you have improved a little bit from the last conversation. At least you said 'good bye' before you hung up on her this time."

"I didn't yell either." Justice announced. It was funny how she counted that an accomplishment.

"Nope, not even a raised voice. Good for you."

"Thank you." Justice smiled. "Has she been calling you too?" justice had to know.

Jane hesitated, but then figured that she would need to know the truth. "Yes Justice, I have been talking to her each day, and telling her how we've been getting along. However, I never told her about the incident in case you were wondering."

Justice had been.

"I know she really does care about you, no matter what you might think." Jane looked over at Justice.

"Maybe. I just don't know though."

"Well, maybe someday you will see all that she has done for you."

"Possibly." Justice agreed. That was all she really wanted to say on the matter though.

Chapter Ten
Whispers Revealed

She was locked in the room. There was only a very small window. And it was raining outside. No light was coming through. The little girl hated the dark, but she had been stuck in this dark, cold room for over two days now. Her mother was gone, and she had no idea where she was, and when she was coming back. Her stomach hurt, and her mouth was so dry that it was hard to swallow. She hadn't been fed since she was thrown in here. Her mother had dumped her in, after she had beaten her. The little girl was covered with bruises from angry fists. She stood up, and began banging on the door, crying and crying, begging for somebody to let her out. The room was dirty, and she could hear rats crawling through the walls. She was afraid of rats. They had evil little eyes, and nasty little tails. Even her mommy was afraid of them. She saw a spider scurry across the floor and let out a scream. Where was her mommy? Why wouldn't she let her out? She was tired, and hungry, but she wouldn't sit down. She kept banging on the door. Begging for somebody to let her out. Maybe her daddy would come home and let her out. As scary as her daddy seemed, he never once hit her, only mommy. He would let her out, then he would go back to where he always stayed. With a sinking feeling the little girl knew that wouldn't happen and nobody would come for her. She would die in this little room, and the rats would scurry all over her. She started crying harder at the thought. Suddenly the ground started shaking, and the walls began closing in. The little girl ran to the door and continued to bang on it. She heard voices, and screamed for them "let me out, please let me out!"

Justice opened her eyes, and saw Valley's worried face leaning over her. "Justice! Wake up, wake up!"
She was saying. Her face looked pale in the moonlight that was streaming though her window, in her sleep she had grabbed the curtains, and they had come tumbling down. That noise, and the noise of her screaming was what had woken Valley up.
"Valley." She started. "I'm awake, I'm awake."
"You were screaming Justice!" Valley announced wide eyed. "Did you have a nightmare?"
Justice thought about it for a minute, and decided she should admit it. "It was just a bad dream."
"That's what a nightmare is." She stated matter-of-factly.
"Whatever, yeah same thing." Justice mumbled.
Valley hopped on the bed. "You still seem scared."
"I'm not scared...I'm just trying to get back to sleep."
"You don't look tired to me, you look scared."
"Whatever. I'm sorry I woke you up. Good night."
But Valley didn't stop. She settled on Justice's bed, and announced, "Mommy, said that when you have a nightmare, you should tell somebody about it, so that it will go away. She said that it makes you feel better."
Although she had never actually tried it, Justice announced that it never worked for her, that she always got them again.
"Well, maybe you should tell me about your nightmare. Just try it again."
"I don't know Valley. It might scare you. "Justice sat up, and

tried to reason Valley to go away. It was the first time Valley had really acknowledged her, and Justice couldn't wait for her to go away. Strange how things worked out.

"No it won't. It was just a dream."

Justice sighed, and wished that it *were* just a dream. Part of her wanted to tell Valley, but the other part of her thought she was too young to understand or care. Then again, Valley had things in her past that were painful too. Maybe she would understand a little bit. "Okay." Justice announced quietly. "I'll tell you about my dream, and why I always have them, if you tell me about Vanessa."

Valley looked shocked, and even a little mad. "I can't tell you that. Vanessa wouldn't like it, and you're not very nice to her."

Justice tried to think of something to say to that. "Valley, how could I be mean to her, if I've never met her? "

Valley looked at Justice and then started to cry, "I can't tell you about her."

Justice nodded. "It's okay," she said. "I know what happened. Vance told me. I was just hoping that maybe you would want to tell me a little more about her. Vance said that you two were close."

Valley nodded her head. "Yeah we were. She was my best friend. I loved my sister, but now she's not here and I miss her. Why can't she come back Justice?" Justice really didn't know what to say. She was very new with the whole 'heaven' concept, but she remembered Jane saying it usually calmed Valley down. "Well." She started. "Isn't she in heaven? Your mom told me about heaven and just thinking about it, makes me want to go there. "She paused. "You know Valley, if I was there, I really don't think I would want to come back. I would want to stay there forever and ever."

"But wouldn't she want to come back and see me?" Valley asked through her tears.

Justice felt her heart ache for this girl. She could feel her pain. "She does want to see you, but she wants you to come up to heaven and see her there someday. Your mom said that one day you will see her again, and you will live with her forever. Maybe Vanessa is waiting for you there." Justice smiled. "Maybe she made new friends, and right now she's telling them all about her little sister named Valley." Justice started to choke up, and she wanted desperately to do anything else than cry. However it was making Valley stop crying. So she continued. "She is telling them that they will all get to meet you someday, and they are all excited.

Valley looked up at Justice. "Do you really think she has friends?" she asked wide-eyed.

"Why not? Isn't heaven supposed to be a happy place? It wouldn't be too happy if you were up there all alone. So she must have friends."

Valley thought that over and said "Yeah. I bet she does."

Valley's face crinkled and another tear slipped down her eye, as she said. "But I miss her a lot. I want to see her now." Justice didn't know what else to say. So she did something she never thought she was capable of: she gave Valley a hug. A long hug, and to her surprise Valley hugged her back.

Finally Justice blurted out "I have an older brother somewhere in the world. I haven't seen him since I was about five, but I know he's out there somewhere." Valley stopped crying and asked, "Why don't you know where he is?"

"Because, they placed us in different foster homes, and split us up. I actually have a lot of siblings, but I don't know where any of them are. My brother and I were close though. He's two years older than me. "Justice paused. "He finally got adopted, but I don't even know who adopted him. I lost contact." Valley saw tears in Justice's eyes. "What's his name?" she asked.

"Sam, Samuel, but I always called him Sam." She stuttered.
"That's a nice name." Valley said, as she brushed away Justice's tears. Valley wasn't crying at all anymore. She was focused on Justice, and Justice was shocked at her compassion. Valley was only nine, but right now she could have passed for older. Justice knew then, that she could tell Valley something that she had never spoken about to anyone else. "Do you still want to know what my dream was about?"

Valley nodded.

"Well when I was a little girl, my parents didn't care about me." Valley looked pretty shocked at that.

"Sometimes I dream about them. I dream about my mom hitting me, or locking me up in a closet for days."

Valley looked at her sadly. "How old were you?"

"Almost four. A social worker came to our house, and let me out of the closet. I guess he figured that I had been pretty abused by my parents. Abused and neglected."

"No wonder you have nightmares." Valley said with wide eyes. "My mommy said that some mommies and daddies aren't good, but I never knew that yours weren't."

"Well, that's why I'm living with you. Because your family is nice, and are letting me stay with them"

"I'm sorry I was mean to you." Valley suddenly said.

Justice laughed, "It's okay. I wasn't as nice to you as I could have been. What do you say, should we be friends from now on?" Justice asked her.

Valley smiled. "Yeah."

Valley went back to her room after that, and Justice actually drifted off to sleep again. She didn't wake up until morning.

Jane went grocery shopping, and Bill and Vance were gone as usual. It was just Justice and Valley. Justice decided that maybe she could get the cereal bowls out and…she thought about trying to fix a breakfast but she really didn't have that much experience cooking. So she just got the cereal out and set it on the counter. She ate breakfast by herself. It seemed very strange to not have the rest of the Carter family here. They usually had a pretty busy breakfast. She finished, washed and rinsed her bowl, and then went into the living room. Maybe she could read some more of Anne of Green Gables. She was really starting to like that book. Anne really did have a big temper, and Justice had laughed at several different parts of the book. Some things she could relate to and other things were just Anne. It was a really good read.

She read for quite a while, as Valley came down and had breakfast.

"Justice Can I show you something?" Valley asked, as she walked into the living room.

Justice closed her book and said, "Sure. What do you want me to see?"

"It's not here, it's somewhere else."

"Okay." She paused. "Where is it?"

"I have to get dressed first, and then I'll show you."

Justice nodded. Valley ran up the stairs and slammed her door. Justice cringed at the bang. Minutes later she was back, with shoes in her hand. "It's outside." She explained.

"Oh." Justice replied, so she got her own shoes.

When they were ready to go, Justice wrote a little note to Jane, in case she got home before they did. She wrote that Valley had something important to show her, and they wouldn't be gone long. She grabbed the spare key and closed the door.

Valley walked beside her. "See that hill?" She pointed. Justice squinted against the bright sunlight. She could just make out a big hill. It had a ton of trees, and looked pretty shady up there.

She wished that she was out of the sun. "Yeah I see it," she said to valley.

"Well that's where we are going."

Justice shrugged "Okay."

They walked up there in silence. It took about fifteen minutes to actually get to the hill, and another ten to climb it. It was bigger than it seemed at first, Justice realized. When they finally reached the top, they were surrounded by trees. Bright Green leaves blocked out the hot sun, making the inside of the little forest quite cool. Valley walked in front and led the way. They walked along a trail and Valley would point out poison Ivey along the path, so Justice wouldn't step on it. She pointed out all of the trees, and Justice was surprised at all of the long names she had memorized. "Wow, you really know your trees."

"Vanessa taught me their names ." Valley replied.

"Oh." Justice looked around "Did she come up here often?"

Valley stopped at a little opening in the forest. A single ray of sun broke through the branches, and illuminated a big headstone, decorated with flowers, and plants.

"She loved it up here. She came all the time." Valley pointed at the gravestone. "So we held the funeral up here, and buried her."

Justice knelt by the grave, and smelled the beautiful flowers. She read the words inscribed on the headstone.

Vanessa Lynn Carter
Beloved daughter and sister.
She will live on in our hearts
FOREVER
January 21 1990 - June 15 2003

Justice just stared at the grave. Vanessa would have been almost the exact same age she was. No wonder Valley had felt like Vanessa was being replaced. "Wow she must have been a wonderful sister." Justice whispered. "Thanks for showing me Valley."

"Yeah sure. I just wanted you to know where she was…where her grave was. Since your part of the family now."

Justice smiled. "Man, I bet she would have loved it up here right now."

"She loved it up here in the summer, it was her favorite time to come."

Justice stood up and looked around. It was really beautiful how that one single ray lit up the grave. The rest of the forest was dim, but that light lit the place up. The wind blew, and green leaves fell like rain. She could hear birds singing, and see squirrels scurrying along the forest. The trees were big. Maybe even the biggest trees she'd seen in her life. She walked back into the middle of the forest to explore a little. Valley was busy picking wild flowers to put on her sister's grave. Justice skipped along the quiet forest, and hummed a little tune to herself. If any of her friends saw her now, they would think she was high. That wasn't it at all. She was at peace. More so than she had ever been. She saw an old wooden swing hanging from a big oak tree, and started towards it. Remembering about the poison Ivey Valley had warned her about, she picked her way carefully. She came up to the old swing and turned it over. She wanted to make sure the wood wasn't rotten, and no bugs had decided to call it home. Thinking she would rather take a chance, Justice sat gently down on the seat and gave a little push. It swung like it had never stopped. Justice glanced upwards to check out the ropes, and saw that they still looked intact. Maybe Valley came up here to swing once in a while. She pumped her legs, higher and higher, enjoying the feeling of freedom. The air was cool and breezy. Her hair was blowing. She felt great in the forest. Justice almost never wanted to leave. Valley came bounding up the path and laughed at Justice on the swing. "Daddy put that swing up for Vanessa one year for her birthday. We would come up here and swing a lot. In fall we use to rake up all the leaves, and then jump off the swing into them. It was fun."

Justice jumped off the swing, "Whoa!" She said with a thump, as she landed on the ground. Luckily she did land on her feet.

"Let me do it." Valley took the swing and swung herself high. She jumped off, and landed with practiced perfection.

"And that was the amazing Valley Carter!" Justice yelled, "Performing live, in the woods."

Valley laughed. "Vanessa use to swing me really hard, and I would go really high."

"Like this?" Justice asked coming up behind her and giving her a hard shove."

"Woohoo! Yeah!" Valley laughed. They spent several hours together just playing around on Vanessa's old wooden swing. It was more fun than Justice could remember having in a long time. They laughed and cheered and played around for a few hours, until Justice realized that they had been gone for a while, and Jane might be worried.

"We better go. Your mom might be getting worried."

"Okay." Valley hopped off the swing, and they headed out of the woods, and down the hill.

Fifteen minutes later, they were back in the house. Jane's car was back in the driveway, and Justice knew that she must have been home for a while. They walked in, and saw Jane putting the rest of the groceries away.

"There you two are. Justice, I saw your note but I had no idea where you guys were."

"Well, I didn't exactly know either. Valley just told me that she wanted to show me something, so I went along."

Valley nodded to confirm it. "I showed her the hill, and Vanessa's grave."

"Oh." Jane looked a little worried. "Was she okay?" She whispered to Justice, as she watched Valley run up the stairs.

"Yeah, she just really wanted to show me the hill."

Jane shook her head in amazement. "That is really something. One day she's shy, and the next day she wants you to be her best friend!"

"Well, we had a talk last night." Justice admitted. "We decided that it would be best if we get along while I'm here."

"Well very good. I'm glad that's over with now." Jane smiled. "She really can be a sweet girl…"

"I know. I saw that today. We were having a lot of fun on the swing."

Jane laughed, "Yeah, well that was Vanessa's and Valley's favorite thing to do."

"I didn't really know that she was so close to my age." Justice looked down. "I kind of realized how she might think I was replacing her sister."

"It was really hard to lose her. We all still miss her, and I don't think we will ever stop. However, we are so glad that we know we will see her again someday. That's what keeps us going."

Justice nodded. "Yeah I can see how it would."

"Justice, have you ever thought about where you would go when you die?" Jane asked slowly.

Justice knew that this conversation would come up someday, since it was a preacher family and all. The problem, was how to get out of it. "Not really." That wasn't so bad, now was it? Although it was a straight lie…at least she had it over with.

"Yeah right." Jane smirked. "I doubt that."

"I don't know what would happen, but I don't like to think about death…it's kind of depressing."

"You never think about heaven or hell?"

"Sure, doesn't everybody?"

"I would imagine so." Jane really didn't know how to go about this. It wasn't going to be an easy conversation, she could already tell. Maybe Bill had better take over this one.

Valley ran into the room, and begged, "Justice play a board game with me please!"

Glad for the interruption, Justice said, "Yeah, okay."

"Can we play my favorite game?" Valley asked, all bright eyed.

"Sure." Justice thought about that for a second. "What is your favorite game?"

"Monopoly!"

"Junior?" *Please say junior.*

"No, the regular one silly." Valley smiled, pulled out the game and began to set it up.

"Great." She tried to sound enthusiastic. Monopoly lasted forever. She was going to be here for a long time

"I'll give you a lunch break in a few minutes." Jane smiled encouragingly. "Valley may love this game, but she still has an appetite."

True to her word, Jane prepared sandwiches for them a half hour later, and they munched on theirs. Vance came home early so he ate with them and then insisted on playing monopoly too. Of course Valley wanted to start all over for Vance, so that's pretty much what they did the rest of the day. When the game finally did end, Justice was relieved. "Oh and guess what Thursday night is?" Vance asked.

"What?" Justice asked.

"It's family game night!" He laughed.

"Ha, very funny Vance."

But Vance was all seriousness now. "No really it is. It's my turn to choose the game too. Lucky for you, Valley's turn was last

Thursday. However, I really do like monopoly."

Justice shot him a look of death, and then laughed. "Oh, I know what this is about. Your just upset that you lost. Huh?" Justice had actually won in monopoly, but not by much. Valley was really good at her beloved game.

"Hey you know, let's see how good you are at clue."

Justice laughed. "I don't think I've played that since I was really little."

Vance let out an evil laugh "Then you shall fall under my demise!"

Justice just laughed and shook her head. "Your nuts, did you know that? I can't believe your family hasn't squashed you by now."

"I'm surprised that *you* haven't squashed me by now."

"Yeah that's surprising to me too. I guess I've just been pretty compassionate lately."

"Must be it."

Vance was right on, and after dinner the dishes were cleared and cleaned. Clue was spread out on the table, and all of the little figures were put in their rightful places. Valley insisted on being Ms. Scarlet and Vance was happy being Colonel Mustard. Justice thought she might like to be Professor Plum. Purple wasn't such a bad color. The game started. Bill and Jane laughed at Justice's and Vance's playful banter.

Every once in a while Vance would state that he knew where the crime was committed, and Justice would shoot back "But, do you know what the murder weapon was?" They would go back to the game with a ferocious fury to win.

The game ended, and it was Bill who won. "Sorry guys," he said, and laughed. "But we know who the real detective in the family is." Jane laughed.

While they were packing up the game, Bill asked Justice" Do

you think maybe you would like to get ice cream with me tomorrow?"

Justice thought it was funny. She felt like a little kid. She always had friends whose parents would take them out for an ice cream after soccer games, or would want to spend time with them, throwing a Frisbee at the park. She just never thought she would be one of the lucky kids who got that. "Sure." She replied with a smile.

Bill looked happy. "Great, then we'll go after dinner tomorrow night."

Justice smiled and started to walk upstairs.

"Oh and Justice," Jane called after her.

Justice spun around.

"You get to choose the game next time."

"Alright, and I'll make sure it's something I'm good at, so Vance doesn't stand a chance."

"I heard that." Vance called from his room.

They all retired to their rooms. Justice couldn't help thinking, as she turned out the lights and crawled under her blankets, that she had never been so happy. There was really something special about this family. Something that might even be able to tame a wild beast such as she.

Chapter Eleven
An Unlikely Bond

Jane took Justice out to get a driver's ed booklet. It had everything in it and Justice knew that this was the first step in convincing Susan that she really wanted to drive and could be responsible enough to handle it. They got back into the car after the DMV and Jane asked, "So what do you have to prove before Susan will let you get your permit?"

"Well, I'll have to prove that I won't be an aggressive driver, which she is convinced that I will be, and I think if I show my devotion to studying, then maybe she might take me seriously."

"Devotion to studying?"

"No shocker there right? School was never in my top priorities."

Now Jane hadn't given much thought to that, since it was Summer and all, but she did have to ask, "What grade are you going into?"

Justice grimaced a little. "The usual, you know…"

Jane could tell that she didn't want to tell her, but she still pressed the issue. "Come on be honest."

"Okay, *honestly* I don't know. I haven't exactly been going to school everyday since…well, eighth grade… at least I think it was eight grade…maybe it was seventh?"

"What do you mean?"

"I've never stuck around for finals and I miss at least three days a week, and occasionally a good week, here and there. So I've managed to make it into the right grade, by being tested and passing…barely."

"So your going into you Junior year?"

"Well, I really didn't stick around too much last year. I don't know if I'll be able to pass or not."

Jane groaned. "What does Susan say about your absences?"

"She yells, and asks if I want to be labeled a 'loser' in life. She's tried many times to change my mind about ditching, but she can't really do it."

"Well, I don't approve either Justice."

Justice kept quiet, because she didn't want to say that if she had the Carter's for a foster family a long time ago, a lot of things would have been different.

"Maybe I'll call Susan when we get home." Jane said after a small pause. "You know, put in a good word."

Justice smiled, "That would be great."

Justice spent a lot of her day pouring over her driver's ed book. Learning the rules of the road didn't seem that hard, and she knew that within a week she would know most of them. She would be able to take her permit test. If Jane or Susan would take her. It would probably be Susan, because she was still her 'legal guardian' until adoption. Adoption. That was a word she never even dreamed of. Sometimes it was just a mere idea, that one could be 'adopted'. Justice thought about the conversation with Jane earlier. She said that she agreed with Susan. Was it possible that maybe…just maybe Susan was right? Justice thought about the possibility. She had never really believed that she would be adopted, yet she constantly skipped school. She would be eighteen in two years, and then she really wouldn't have to stay with the agency anymore. But then where would she go? Justice didn't know how she had managed to miss this part. If she continued on the path she was on, then she wouldn't be eligible for college, and there was no way in the world that she would have money to attend. Then again if she had devoted her time to studying, instead of hanging out with her friends, then maybe she would have been able to get a scholarship. You never know. Maybe she would have some privileges since she was a foster kid. Then she shook her head again. What had she been thinking all these years? She had wanted so badly to be disconnected from the agency forever, yet all this time she was really chaining herself to it. What did she expect to happen after she turned eighteen anyway? To suddenly get granted a wish by a fairy godmother and all of a sudden get a house, a car, job, and money? There was no way she would be able to support herself with a job from McDonalds. "All these years wasted..." Justice thought bitterly.

 The Carter's were a nice family, and Justice could happily imagine herself forever with them. She wouldn't get her hopes up though. There really wasn't a reason to. She had felt like this before. That one family all those years back. It wasn't long after she had been in foster care that a nice family had come and taken her to their home...

 At first she was nervous because she didn't know who the lady with the big auburn hair was, the guy she was with, was huge, and she thought he looked like a grizzly bear. They took her to their house, and showed her around. They let her play with a whole bunch of toys that their eighteen-year-old daughter use to have. They told her that she was away at collage. They were kind to her, and never yelled, or smacked her. For the first time the little girl felt safe. They did many things together for years. Although they never officially 'adopted' her. She knew that they would one day. They loved her, and even said so. They just couldn't cover the cost financially for a while. That was okay though, because she was pretty much their daughter anyway.

Justice snapped out of her memories. Lately, she had been having nightmare, after nightmare, and now she was starting to day-dream about things that she had refused to let herself dwell on. Most of the time she denied that she had ever been happy when she was young. The memories were coming back though. All of the ones that she had tried to forget all of these years. Good ones, and many bad ones. Justice suddenly grabbed her head.

"I don't want to remember." She whispered harshly, and swore. "Go away, don't come back!"

She opened her eyes and grabbed at her driver's ed book. She had to concentrate on something else. Scanning the pages quickly she tried to memorize all of the street signs. She read faster, and faster trying with everything she had to forget, and force the painful memories out. She wanted to scream, and tear them out. Never. She never wanted to remember them. They never happened, it was a lie. She told herself that her memories were all lies that the agency had made up to make her unhappy. A knock on the door made her jump. Valley opened. "Time for dinner." She announced and left as quickly as she came. Valley hadn't noticed that she was distressed. Good. Maybe Jane wouldn't either or the rest of the Carter's for that matter.

Dinner went smooth, Justice helped Jane clear the table, while Bill changed into shorts and a tee shirt.

Bill walked into the kitchen and asked if Justice was all set. "Yep, I'm ready when you are." She replied.

So off they went. Bill bragged along the way about the little ice cream parlor they were going to. He said it was the best ice cream around, and that she would love it. Justice agreed that it probably was, and answered any questions he threw at her. When they got there, they ordered. "Okay what do you want Justice, my treat."

"Hmmm… well what are you going to get?"

Bill thought a moment and then said, "I think I want a banana split. They are delicious, but it's hard for even me to finish one." He patted his stomach, which only hung slightly over his belt. "I don't know Justice, are you up for the challenge?"

"I think I could give it a shot." Justice smiled.

"We'll have two banana splits." He ordered.

They went to the counter and sat on shiny red stools. Justice looked around, and found that she loved the 50's style ice cream parlor. It was neat. Everything from the checkered floor to the red table tops, had a unique feel to it. Their splits were brought to them, and they wasted no time in plunging into them. Justice pulled the cherry from the top, and popped it into her mouth.

"Justice, how are things going for you?"

"Fine." Justice responded, "I really like your family."

Bill's face lit up. "I'm really glad to hear that. I know we have all enjoyed your company."

Justice didn't know what to say. "Thanks."

"You and Vance look like you are getting along pretty well."

"Yeah, we are. He's a little bit annoying, but it's not so bad."

Bill laughed, "Yep that's Vance for you." He paused. "I noticed that you and Valley are getting along better too."

Justice hadn't actually told Bill, or Jane about the other night when she and Valley finally agreed to get along. At the time she figured that it was mainly between them, and that nobody else would really notice, but apparently they had.

"We had kind of a talk a couple nights ago. Sort of an understanding I guess you could say." Justice knew that Bill and Jane slept through her nightmares. It was a relief to her and she didn't plan on telling them to Bill.

"Really? What did you decide?" He asked the inevitable.

"We just told each other a few things. That's all. explained ourselves."

Bill caught on that it was mainly between them, and Justice didn't want to talk about it at the moment. He quickly said, "Well that's great that you guys are getting along now."

"Yeah." Justice agreed. "Yum you were right about this ice cream, it's the best I've ever had." Justice took a big bite, and felt a contrast between the hot fudge, and cold ice cream.

"See what did I tell ya? Vance, and Valley love it too."

"They could have come along."

"Yeah, but I wanted to get to know you, and ask you a few things. You know it's kind of a foster dad, and foster daughter time."

"Yeah that's cool." Justice shoved another spoon of ice cream in her mouth, and Bill did the same.

It had been a while since he had a teenage girl. He didn't even know what to say! What were they into these days? Cell phones…make-up? Clothes? Boys? Well, skip the boys.

"So I hear you want your permit." He finally blurted out.

"Yeah, I would really like to get it, but it's kind of up to Susan, and of course you guys."

"When is the soonest you would be ready for the test?"

Justice laughed, "At the rate I've studied, probably by next Saturday."

"Well next Saturday it is." Bill announced.

"What!?" Justice exclaimed, "You mean I can get it next Saturday?"

"Yep, your old enough, and I don't see why not."

Justice frowned. "What about Susan?"

"Oh Jane talked to her earlier today. She took care of it."

"She probably had to beg her."

"I don't think it was as hard as you make it out to be." Bill pointed out, "I think Susan just needed to be reassured that you would…"

"Take it seriously?" Justice finished.

"Yeah."

"Should have known, but hey can't really blame her I guess."

Bill laughed at her honesty. "So you really give Susan a hard time huh?"

Justice stared at her ice cream. "I don't really know why. She just really bugs me."

"Are you mad at her Justice?"

Justice thought it over. Susan was one person in her life who she had known for what seemed forever. She was a lot nicer to her when she was younger. But for some reason when she got older, everything about Susan upset her. She remembered the second foster family she was placed with. It seemed years ago. She was twelve at the time. The couple who took her in were terrible. They were mean, and smelled bad. The house was small and cramped, very different from the Johnson's house. The Johnson's house, that had always made her feel tiny, was a stark contrast to the tiny one she was transferred too. She had been angry with Susan for placing her with such a bad foster family. She hadn't even stayed the night. Her first encounter with Janet, Ryan and Greg was that night. Susan had yelled at her, and told her what a dangerous thing running away was. Justice had said some pretty vicious things to Susan. Mainly because she was hurting, and she felt that Susan had no sympathy for her. Was she mad at Susan? Yes, she supposed she was.

"Now that you mention it." She started. "I guess I am. "

"Why?" Bill asked.

"I'm mad because she's put me with the worst families ever,

and dragged me to them each time. I'm sure she hates me. Then she turns around and acts like she cares about me, and that she's always so worried when I sneak off at night. She doesn't get what it's like to be stuck in strange house, with nobody familiar around."

"That's true, she doesn't know what it's like for you, but I would have to say, talking to Susan (and this is just my opinion) I really think she cares about you. I know she gets worried when you sneak out, and she really tries hard to find good families for you. I think she just doesn't know what to do sometimes. She just wanted you to be in a home where you're loved, and can get on with your life."

"Well, she's never proved that she cares about me, that's for sure."

"Why do you think she sent you to us?" Bill asked her point blank. "She obviously cared enough about you to keep you out of the mental home didn't she?"

Justice sighed. Susan told her that the Carter's were her last chance, and if she couldn't deal with them, then there was nothing else she could do, except send her away. "Yeah so she did one thing right. I think it was just because she felt bad about all of the other bad homes she sent me too."

Bill laughed, "I don't know Justice. I really think she cares about you. Maybe one day you will see it."

"Yeah maybe." Justice said bored of the conversation.

"So what did you think about the youth group the other night? Was it really weird to you?" He asked changing the subject again.

" it was a little different. I know you're a preacher and all so no offense, but I'm not really into all of the same stuff. The people were nice though. Vance has some good friends."

"Yes he does, and no offense taken. But if you don't believe in God, then what do you believe in?"

Justice thought a moment before she answered. "I pretty much believe in luck and fate."

"Luck and fate?" Bill questioned.

"Well yeah, how else do you explain my life? If there was a God, then why have I had such a bad life? Isn't your god supposed to be compassioned, lovey dovey and all?"

Bill laughed, "Lovey dovey, huh? God is good Justice, and he is compassionate. Sometimes we don't understand his ways, and I don't pretend to but…"

"Oh yeah, right. "Justice cut in, "He *is* compassionate and he *is* good, yet he makes all these bad things happen. I don't see that as compassionate, and I don't see that as good."

"What I was going to say, was that sometimes really awful things happen. Things that are horrible and we wonder why they happened. I don't know why God allows some things to happen, but I believe he can use any thing bad and turn it into good. "

Justice disagreed. "Well a god who wouldn't help me out back when I really needed him, is not one that I want to deal with now."

Bill thought about it. She was pretty angry at God at the moment, even though she said she didn't believe in his existence. Pretty funny how she was quick to blame him, when just minutes before she had denied him. He had one more thing to say and then he would let her change the subject. "Justice, Jesus loves you and He's waiting for you to come to him."

"Well He's going to have to keep waiting, because I'm not convinced yet." Justice paused. "But It would be kind of nice knowing that someone still loves me after all I've done, and all I've been through."

Bill nodded.

"He just doesn't sound real. Isn't he the same as believing in the tooth fairy, and Santa clause? Sure, they seem really great and all, but it's just a legend. A fairy tale, whatever you want to call it."

"I understand your doubts, when I was your age I was the same way. Sure, my dad was a pastor too, but I couldn't help feeling like Christianity was his religion. I wanted to find my own thing to believe in. "

"What did you do?"

"I tried everything. I tired to be an atheist, and when I mean 'tried' I mean that after a while I realized how stupid it was that nothing made the world, and we were all by chance. It just didn't sit well with me. So I switched to some new age, stuff and became my 'own god'." Bill laughed, "Those are some of the craziest years of my life because there was no right, and there was no wrong. If you don't know where your standards are then you don't know how to act. My buddies and I believed that good, and bad were just words, and that everybody defined their own good and bad. Therefore, whenever I did something bad, I told myself that it was actually good in my new belief. Even through those dark times though, I could feel God speaking to me, trying to pull me back to him. One day, I just cracked. My life was a mess, and I realized how bad it had really become. I needed God, and he was there for me. I came back to him that day, and he accepted me. I had never felt so much joy." Bill stopped.

Justice was staring into her empty ice cream bowl. "Wow, I always thought pastors were holy from birth or something."

Bill had to laugh, "No one's perfect Justice, even pastors." He chuckled. "Everybody has temptations. All of us sin everyday. But when we ask God to forgive us, he wipes the slate clean."

Justice nodded. "That's pretty crazy."

"Yeah it is. But I am sure glad he does."

Justice started to feel a little uncomfortable. She really hadn't heard to much about God in her life, but what Bill had just told her didn't seem so bad. It reminded her of the other night when she snuck out. The Carter's forgave her. They wiped the slate clean. They still seemed to like her the same as when they had first met her. It was nice knowing that somebody would care so much.

"Hey you finished your ice cream." Bill looked shocked. "I think Vance could only finish his once."

Justice laughed, "Yeah well now we have another competition to work on."

"Well we better get going."

Justice could see that he had finished his ice cream too. They left, and on the way home Bill announced that he was glad she came along. Justice realized that she was glad that she had come too, and not just for the ice cream. She had found something in common with a pastor. Bill, had known what it was like to feel doubt, and he went through some hard times too. Justice could relate to that, and she couldn't get over the fact that she had just befriended a pastor. *Now that is an unlikely bond.* Justice thought to herself.

They got home, and Jane was passing out cake. "now I know you just had ice cream but there is plenty…"

"Oh no, really I can't eat another thing!' The sight of the cake was making her feel sick. Okay, so maybe she wouldn't eat so much next time.

Jane laughed, "I guess you got the famous banana split huh?"

Vance was at the counter eating a piece of chocolate cake. "Oh no, you didn't finish it did you?"

Justice nodded. "Afraid I did."

Valley was sitting at the table and let out a gasp. "Wow Vance she beat you! You finished yours on the third time you got it. Justice finished hers the first time!"

"I can tell." Vance laughed. "She looks like she's about to throw up." Then he let out a devious grin. "Say Justice, do you want to see if you can eat a double split? We can go tomorrow with Wiley and the gang, and have a competition. Should be great..."

"Vance..."

"No really. I'm sure you would *love* more vanilla ice cream, with all of that hot fudge..."

Justice could feel her stomach moving. "Okay, I am so full. That is the last thing I want to hear."

"Well you must want some more, come on."

Justice laughed, "Good try, but there is no way I can eat anymore ice cream for at least a year."

Everyone was doing their own thing. Jane was sitting in the living room on a couch reading, Valley was playing in her room, and Vance and Bill were watching some sports channel, in the living room that Justice had no idea what was going on. She was about to go take a bath when the phone rang. Seeing as everybody else was busy, Justice went to answer it.

"Hello?"

"Hi, is this Justice?"

"Yeah. Is this Susan?"

"I saw one of your friends walking around town today. As a thought, I decided that I would ask her if she had seen you lately."

Her heart stopped. Was it possible that Susan knew about the other night? The Carter's had kept it to themselves, so she knew they really wouldn't have told. Did...?

"Who did you talk to?" Justice asked casually, denying any guilt in her voice.

"Janet, and you know what she told me? She said that on Tuesday night you snuck out of your window and came to see them at the bar. She said that you were there for hours. She had no idea how you got home."

Justice's mind erupted in fury. Janet! She should have known. Of course she hadn't said a word about her little part on the whole matter. About how she lied to her, and convinced her to come out of the window. Justice took her responsibility for the other night, but she sure didn't need Janet causing trouble. What did she say? What could she say? She really couldn't lie and say that she didn't sneak out, but if she admitted it, then Susan would get mad, and possibly place her with another family. What if she got mad at the Carter's for not reporting to her, and took her out of the family? Suddenly that new fear seemed real, and Justice realized that she couldn't let that happen. She wasn't going to be taken from the Carter's and she wasn't going to let Janet ruin her life.

"You know Janet's always hung over, and you know that half of what she says is gossip. She probably heard that I was out from other people who 'claimed' that they saw me. I think she was just trying to cause you to worry."

Susan sounded really angry as she said, "Yeah right. Justice I know you were out the other night. It would be just like you to take advantage of the Carter's kindness. How could you?"

Justice lost her temper. She was getting nervous about the whole situation, and she was willing to say anything to change Susan's mind. "Would you just shut up? Why would Janet betray me to you? Huh? You know that we're good friends. There is no way in the world that she would rat me out. You should know that by now."

Justice was going to use her old friendship with Janet to get her out of this one. There had to be a way out.

"Justice I'm trying to help you find a home, but I don't understand you! I don't know why you do what you do, maybe you can try to help me out... I think I'm going to call that psychologist back. He told me that you would pull a stunt like this. I should have listened..."

"No, Susan wait." She tried to keep the desperation from seeping into her voice. "Okay, I admit. I did sneak out the other night, I got home because Ryan drove me home. The Carter's woke up and found out that I snuck out, but we talked about it, and the Carter's gave me a second chance. I'm serious they really did."

"I just don't buy it Justice."

"You have to buy it, it's the truth!" Justice screamed. She walked up stairs and then back down them, with the cordless phone in hand. Anyone who saw her would think she looked like an angry tiger pacing back and forth, ready to attack. Justice walked into the kitchen and sat on a stool. Susan was lecturing her, but Justice could tell what she was about to say next.

"So that is why..." Susan went on and on.

"Ask Jane if you don't believe me!" Justice screamed angrily. "Ask her! She gave me a second chance, and now your trying to throw it away!"

"Justice you just shouldn't be in a foster home right now, it's not the best place for you to be. You are to unstable!"

"I'm not going to let you ruin this for me, I'm not leaving!" Justice jumped off the stool so hard, that it tipped over, and fell to the ground. It landed on her foot, and pain shot through her. Driven by rage, and now pain, she picked up the stool and threw it across the kitchen. It hit with a loud BANG! The stool splintered, and the legs fell off. It had hit the refrigerator. Susan heard the noise on the other side of the phone "What was...?"

"I hate you Susan, I hate you so much!" Justice dropped the phone.

All four of the Carter's rushed in. They saw the mess, and saw Justice drop the phone.

Bill hurriedly grabbed it and asked "Who is this?"

Jane stared wide-eyed at Justice. Her face was red, and her eyes were red. She was a bomb that just exploded.

"Mommy!" Valley pointed at the once brown stool, now turned into fire wood.

"Justice, what is going on? What happened?"

Justice was stuttering and shaking. "I'm sorry, I-I don't know why I threw it…I got so mad…"

"Whose on the phone?" Vance asked Bill.

Bill brought the phone into the living room, and began talking to Susan. Vance followed.

"Susan said she's going to send me away…"

Jane wrapped her arms around Justice. "No she's not honey. No she's not. Did she find out about the other night?"

"Yeah."

"Well this is the reaction I expected from her. She probably feels bad about you sneaking off, and is sorry that she gave you to us. We gave you a second chance and Bill will explain that to Susan. She will understand. Susan doesn't see all the changes in you that we see."

"But you don't know Susan. She's ruthless. She will come and get me and lock me in an asylum forever."

"No, she won't. She wants what's best for you, and she thinks that you are just going to get worse. Bill will tell her that you are getting better, and that you haven't snuck out again."

"But she…"

"No." Jane said firmly. "She really doesn't understand. But she will once Bill explains everything to her." Jane paused. "How did she find about this anyway?"

"Janet. She was the reason why I snuck out the other night.

I know it's no excuse and the fault was mine, but Janet told me that she needed my advice for something. She wanted to talk privately with me."

"What did she want to talk about?" Jane asked.

"If she should get back with her abusive boyfriend. I only went along to help her out. We weren't going to be gone long but she tricked me! They were already back together. I told her that I never wanted to go in the first place, so she told me a lie to get me to come." Justice looked down. "Now she betrayed me again. She told Susan about the other night. I thought Janet was my best friend, now I see differently." Justice's anger died down a little to sadness. "How could I have been so stupid?"

"You weren't Justice. But you were confused." Jane looked at her compassionately. "Everybody needs friends, you maybe need them most. Why didn't you tell me the reason why you snuck out?"

"I didn't want it to seem like an excuse. I knew it wasn't, but I felt so bad about going."

"You don't know how happy I am to hear that." Jane said unexpectedly. "I thought you were unhappy here at first, now I know differently."

Justice couldn't believe her ears. The Carter's never ceased to amaze her. She looked towards the broken stool.

"Wow. I'm sorry about the stool." She got the broom and swept up the splinters.

Vance came back into the room, and gathered up the stool legs. "I think I can fix it," he said. Jane looked at the pieces he held, they did seem like they would fit back together with a little wood work.

"See if you can."

After the splinters were gone, Bill came back into the kitchen and hung the phone up. "I explained the situation. Susan was very upset, but I think she understands now."

"Thank you." Justice told him.

"Try not to throw anymore things okay?"

"You've got my word on that one I'm sorry. I know I need to control my temper more. I will next time."

They all went and sat down in the living room for a family meeting. "Susan asked us to report next time you sneak out." Bill started. "However I told her that you wouldn't be sneaking out anytime soon."

"She's right." Justice confirmed. "I won't. I really don't want to be sent away. I like it here."

The whole family beamed.

"We like you here too." Valley told her. She was sitting right next to her on the couch.

"I'm sorry that I screamed too."

The family announced that it was okay.

"Susan just wants to make sure that you aren't causing more trouble, and that our family is the best one for you."

"But she panicked! She's never been so ready to pull me out of a family before!"

"I agree she did panic a little, but I think she felt bad about putting you with us in the first place, and she didn't really think you would sneak out again after her little talk with you." Bill said,

"Yeah, she thought she really had me with the mental hospital." Justice rolled her eyes. "She did. That's the whole reason I came along. I never really expected to get along with you guys. I was going to run away the first night, but you guys showed me so much kindness…I couldn't leave. For the first time in a long time, I didn't want to."

The Carter's were speechless. Justice was admitting that she wasn't going to give them a chance at first. She was going to run away, but here she was. If this wasn't a miracle, then what was?

"I really didn't come into this giving you guys a fair shot. I came because I didn't want to be sent away, but I've found that I like it here."

Bill laughed, "Now Justice you can't deny that this isn't a God thing. What an unlikely bond."

"Maybe it is a God-thing." Justice admitted. Why not? An unlikely Bond. That was the second time this night that she had heard those words.

Chapter Twelve
Singing a New Tune

Today was going to be a good day. Justice thought to herself. It was Saturday morning and she knew that next Saturday she would be getting ready for her first driving lesson. She couldn't wait. As she walked down the isles picking up the things Jane had asked her to get, she couldn't help thinking about dinner later on. Well okay, to be honest with herself she was only really thinking about Wiley. He was going to be there tonight. What was she going to wear? She would have to ask Vance what kind of restaurant they were going to, so she knew whether to dress nice, or very casual. Wow, was this really her? She never use to care what she wore. Whatever she was wearing at the moment was what was on her when she went anywhere with her other friends. She had to stop calling them her friends. According to the carters, as well as Wiley, they weren't. Well she thought Ryan was. He had really helped her out that one night and he was often the one she talked to when they all got together. He was a pretty nice guy for the most part. He had a hard time too. Ryan was eighteen, and his parents split up when he was twelve. He was really close with his dad, but the court gave custody to his mom. That meant he spent most of his life with his mother, and only saw his dad once in a while. Well, his mom got remarried and his new step dad didn't really want him visiting his biological father anymore, so Ryan wasn't able to visit his dad for years. He was eighteen now, and could legally see who ever he wanted, but the damage had been done. He had gotten into the group, and the bar when he was young, and he had remained close with them ever since. He and Gregg hit it off pretty fast, and Gregg was friends with Janet. They all met, and then she joined it. She was the youngest member of the group, but they all allowed her to join. It was all Janet's doing. Janet. Justice groaned inwardly. Why did Janet have to do this? What had she ever done to her? All along Justice had done everything with her. She went to all of the parties Janet insisted she go to. Even when Justice felt a little awkward. Most of the times she was around people who were at least two years older sometimes more. The wild parties made her a little nervous, but Janet had always dragged her along, as well as Gregg and Ryan. They had stuck together through thick and thin. Shouldn't all of them be the best of buddies like Vance and his friends? Yet here she was, not wanting to see Janet again. She hadn't had a real conversation with Greg in a long time. Ryan was the only one of them so far who showed a little bit of decency. He had been there for her the other night, and that had meant a lot to her. Justice picked up a can of green beans Jane had requested, and walked back down the isles, trying to remember which one Jane was on. She found her on the baking isle with a muffin mix in her hand. "What do you think about Blueberry muffins?" she asked her.

Justice smiled, "Their my favorite other than chocolate chip." She placed the can of green beans in the basket and asked,

"Now what else do you want me to get?"

"Well do want to go find some fresh blueberries? The produce is just over there." She pointed to a refrigerated section with a

PRODUCE sign dangling above it.

So Justice headed over, and picked out a little carton of blueberries. She turned around to head back and bumped into somebody.

"Oh excuse me." She spun around to apologize.

"Hey look who it is." Lacee smiled.

"Hey Lace," Justice gave her friend a hug. "what are you doing bumping into people?"

Lacee laughed. "Actually I was picking up a few things for my folks. What are you doing here?"

"I'm here with my new foster family. Yeah, we are grocery shopping together."

Lacee Stared wide-eyed, "And you're still here! You haven't decided to run off yet, I'm impressed."

Justice chuckled. "Well, you know. They aren't so bad. I kind of like this family."

Lacee jumped up and down, despite the weird stares people around her were giving. "I'm so happy for you! You actually found a foster family you like. That's great Justice."

"Yeah, I'm pretty happy. Is this what you felt like when you got adopted?"

"Yeah. I was so glad to get away from the agency and finally have a home of my own. What does Susan think?"

"Well…" Justice related to her the whole story about her sneaking out, and the phone call. She ended with telling her about Janet.

"Wow." Lacee said when Justice had finished. "You have been busy. I'm so sorry about Janet. That must have been hard."

"You know, I'm not as upset as I thought I would be at first. I guess I kind of knew all along that she wasn't a real friend."

"Yeah." Lacee agreed. "Well whenever you can, come visit me at my new home! I would love to show you around, and you can come and see my parents again."

"I remember them."

Lacee laughed, "I know the remember you too."

Justice had been in a particular bad mood the day they came to pick Lacee up. Justice had been kicked out of a foster house and was waiting in Susan's office, when she saw Lacee. She told her that she was being adopted. Justice had been a little sad, because now she wouldn't be seeing her as often, but she had been happy for her. When Lacee's new parents came in to pick her up, Justice decided it was her chance to slip away quietly. Susan would be sidetracked, she wouldn't notice her slipping away. Well Susan noticed how close she was getting to the door, and asked her to go back to her office. Justice had complied but not before throwing something and causing a riot. She ended her fuss with a slam of Susan's office door. Yeah Lacee's parents had been able to see what kinds of friends Lacee had made all right.

"Yeah they may not want me around."

"I think they'll be able to see that you aren't always that destructive. Just around Susan."

"Well I'm hopefully going to get my permit next week, so maybe I can drive up there!" Justice exclaimed.

"Hey that's great! Then you'll have no excuse not to visit."

After a few more brief words, Justice said goodbye to her friend, and hurried to find Jane. No doubt she had been looking for her. Justice found Jane walking up and down the isles, looking.

"Jane." Justice called.

"She spun at her name, "Oh there you are. I was looking for you."

"Oh yeah, sorry. I got caught up talking to a friend. A good friend. She got adopted not that long ago." She added quickly.

"Oh Okay."

"Here I got the blueberries. They look really good."

"They do, just put them in the basket. I think that's all we need."

So they paid and left the store.

In the car Justice finally had to ask the question that was making her anxious. "Jane, did Vance say where we are going tonight?"

"Yeah he said you guys are going to some restaurant."

"Yeah but do you know which one?"

"No I don't think so, why?"

Justice hesitated. "I just wanted to know what I should wear."

"Oh." Jane was beginning to understand. "Well I don't think it will be too fancy, but if you're worried about it, you can always wear jeans, and one of you church tops. That way you'll look stylish, but not dressy."

Justice nodded. "Okay I'll do that."

"Is there a special someone going tonight?"

Justice blushed a little. "No, not really."

"Like maybe the guy who you started drooling over at the pretzel stand? Or the one who almost ran you over?"

Justice laughed, "Okay, it's a possibility. Did you know who he was when we were at the mall?"

"I had forgotten his face, I'm sorry to say, but I don't know how I did. He and Vance have been friends for a while."

"Oh."

"Yeah, if I had remembered I would have introduced you guys then."

"That's okay." Justice laughed.

Later that night Justice was ready to go, and Vance was goofing off. She was watching the time, but Vance seemed to be watching the TV. He brushed his hair and sprayed on some deodorant, but then walked into the living room, and kicked back.

"Vance I think we should get going now." Justice prodded.

"Huh? Oh yeah." Vance got up. "Well, you look nice." He winked. "I'm sure Wiley will think you look nice too."

"Vance!"

"Okay, Okay."

"Don't say another word."

Vance laughed an evil laugh. "We'll be back later mom!" He yelled.

"Okay have fun!" She yelled back.

Vance pulled into the restaurant and Justice was satisfied. It looked like she was dressed right. Tanika, was dressed in jeans, and a nice shirt too. Wiley was looking as dashing as usual and Justice shot Vance a look before she would get out of the car. "Not a word." She mouthed, and then turned it into a big smile, as she greeted the others.

"Got it." Vance gave an over-exaggerated wink. "Hey Guys, let's get in and get a table I'm starved."

They all followed Vance inside. The waiter showed them a table and they all sat down and started reading the menu. Justice sat next to Tanika, and Vance and Wiley sat across from them. Wiley say directly across from her. *Great.* She couldn't help thinking. *Now every time I take a bite to eat, I'm going to be worried about food dripping on my chin.* She checked her napkin, and gave a slight nod of satisfaction. It was a decent size and it could do the trick with any messy face.

"So how have you been?" Wiley asked her.

He asked me a question! Justice thought giddily. Then realized he *had* so she better answer. "Pretty good. I got another call from Susan yesterday, and she was threatening to send me away, but Bill talked to her. I'm off the hook."

"Well that's good, yeah what made her want to place you somewhere else?"

Justice sighed, but told him the story anyway. He already knew about the sneaking out part, and about Janet, but she related how Janet betrayed her again.

"Yikes, I would say it was a tough day."

"Nothing a bowl of ice cream can't cure." Vance teased.

Justice made a face, but laughed, "I think you're just jealous that I finished the banana split on my first try. According to your sister, it took you three times."

Wiley laughed," you were able to finish it? That's pretty good. Yeah. Vance and I were practicing for a while."

Vance laughed. "I keep telling her that we need to see who can finish a double first."

"I think we should see we should meet that challenge after dinner. What do you guys say?" Wiley asked.

They were all game so, it was agreed.

The restaurant was an Italian one, so they decided on a pizza. They ordered four root bears and two pepperoni pizzas.

When the waiter left, Vance suggested they go around the table and each say their favorite hobbies, sort of as an icebreaker.

Tanika went first. "Well, I love to sing and dance. I've been taking dance lessons since I was five, and started singing in choir when I was nine. Other than that I like to paint, and draw."

"She has an amazing voice." Wiley said. "I liked that song you sang last year for Christmas. It was great."

Tanika smiled her thanks, and then looked at Justice. "Well I don't really know…I haven't ever taken any sports before, or dance, or choir." She laughed. "I like to sing in the shower, explore woodsy places, and hang out with friends." She thought a moment. "I guess if escaping was a hobby that would be the thing I do the most." They all laughed.

"I don't know, I can see you doing well in drama." Vance announced. "Have you ever taken any acting classes before?"

"I was a lead in the school musical when I was in sixth grade."

"What was the musical?"

Justice laughed, "Annie. I had to wear a red curly wig and everything."

They all laughed at the image. Then it was Wiley's turn.

"I play the guitar. I've been playing for a few years now, and that's pretty much what I do. I also like whooping Vance in basketball. That's always fun." He grinned. Vance laughed out loud and muttered a "You wish." Wiley continued, "I also like photography. One of my weirdest obsessions is taking pictures during a storm."

"Yeah there was this one time we had a really bad storm, and we had all these tornado warnings, and there goes Wiley out in the middle of the storm, snapping pictures." Tanika rolled her dark eyes. "We all thought you were going crazy."

They erupted in laughter again, and then Vance went. "I like fixing my car, adding to it, polishing it…my car is my hobby, my life, my passion…"

"Yeah, yeah we get it." Justice cut in.

Vance smiled. "Okay fine, yeah I love working on my car, and shooting hoops, and killing Wiley in football." Wiley slugged Vance in the arm. The pizzas were delivered before they could hit each other anymore, and the guys dove in. Tanika and Justice waited until they were done filling their plates before they grabbed their slices.

"Aren't they rude?" Tanika asked Justice, then she laughed, "They act like they're starved to death."

"We are." Vance announced. "We haven't eaten since our late lunch."

Justice smirked. "Don't eat too much Vance, I would hate for you to lose the ice cream challenge."

"Oh yeah, got to save room for that."

The four finished their pizza, and continued talking for a while. Vance called for the check, and they each threw in a few bills.

They all headed over to the 50's ice cream parlor afterwards. All four of them ordered the double banana split, and claimed a table. As they sat down with their banana splits, Justice smelled, the thing that she had conquered last night, only this time it looked much bigger.

"Are you ready for this?" Vance asked. All three of them nodded. "On your mark, get set, go!"

They all started to eat their ice cream quickly. It must have looked funny for the other people sitting around. Four older teens each acting like little kids. It was fun though. Justice pushed spoon after spoonful of cold ice cream into her mouth. Every once in a while she would glance in Vance's bowl to see how he was doing. They were tied at the moment. Vance glanced in Justice's bowl and let out a groan, "Man you're fast."

Tanika's bowl was probably the most full, and she was shaking her head, "I don't think I can finish this, I'm not even going to try to win."

It was between three now.

Ten minutes had passed, and Justice was really beginning to feel full. Vance and Wiley were still going, so she had to as well.

Vance started waving his hands excitedly, as he realized he only had a few bites left. Justice could tell he had one or two bites less than she did, so she shoved bigger spoonfuls into her mouth. Tanika was laughing hysterically at them. Suddenly Wiley sat up, and placed his spoon in his ice cream bowl, and wiped his face. "Keep going guys, keep going." He cheered.

Vance and Justice stopped, and looked. Wiley had licked his bowl clean. He beat them fair and square.

"Aw good one, Wiley. Ruin my chance of winning."

Wiley laughed. "I guess I'm the ice cream champ!"

"But second place is still open." With that Vance poured the remainder of ice cream into his mouth, and gulped it down.

"Second!"

Justice laughed, "Okay fine! I'll give it to you. You gulped that last bite pretty fast, and I've been full since five minutes ago." She pushed the bowl aside.

"I think we need a picture of this moment as I, Wiley Taylor, am the ice cream champ. "He took a picture with all four of them.

"Justice groaned. No more ice cream for me. I thought I was done yesterday, but aw man, I am REALLY done now."

"Yeah I bet." Tanika laughed. "I can't wait to tell Emily about this one."

Tanika looked at the time, and announced, "Well I better get home. My parents will be expecting me."

"I'll walk you to you car." Vance walked outside.

"You're pretty fast Justice, I have to admit." Wiley announced.

"Well you won, fair and square. I honestly will never touch ice cream again."

He laughed, "Yeah I'm done for a while too. So how long will you be here for, or do you know?"

Justice sobered. "I don't know. Hopefully for a while, but it just depends."

"On what?"

She hesitated. She didn't really want to say it, she never liked admitting it, but yet… "How long the Carter's foster me for. I really don't know. There's always the possibility of the Carter's adopting me but…" She frowned.

"What?" Wiley asked gently.

"Well, there's also a possibility that Susan will find another home…I don't think it's very likely, but if she found somebody to adopt me, then I would be handed over to that person for a while, or until they try to adopt me. The Carter's are just my emergency foster home. I could really be transferred any time."

"That's pretty scary."

"Yeah. I mean, it's not like I haven't been transferred before, but I've never been adopted."

"Have you ever been close?" Wiley asked, he knew he was asking a big question, but maybe she would open up a little, and tell him.

"When I was almost five, I was taken to this family. The Johnson's." She paused. "They were really nice, and they wanted to adopt me really bad. They told me they couldn't because of financial reasons, but that wasn't the real reason." She shook her head. "Susan told me later, it was because my parents refused to give me up for adoption. In other words, they wouldn't sign the necessary papers. I have eight other siblings, and they are all adopted now. Most of them were given up for adoption, except for my brother and me. My mom wouldn't give us up. My brother was taken into foster care earlier on, because he had asthma, and my mom wasn't taking care of him well. She had no choice in that, but she wouldn't sign the adoption papers until a couple years later."

Wiley shook his head, at the cruelty she and her brother had suffered.

"My mom and dad said they wouldn't let anybody take me away either, so it took them four years to get me out of that awful home, and into foster care." Justice stopped. She shouldn't be talking about this. Not now. She could feel the anger rising, and she felt a cold chill run down her spine. She was afraid. She didn't want to talk anymore.

Wiley sensed something, and said. "You don't have to say

anything if you don't want to. I know it must be painful."

"Okay, then I think I'm going to stop now." Justice blurted.

"Thanks for trusting me with that." Wiley said.

"You're the first person I've ever told that too. Other people know, but not by me telling them."

Vance walked back in, and asked "Is something wrong? You guys look so serious."

Wiley glanced at Justice. She erupted into a smile, "Nope, not at all." Wiley took the queue, and said, "Well I had a lot of fun tonight you guys. We should do this again sometime."

"Yeah." Justice said, "We should." They all walked out to their cars, and Justice spotted a familiar spot. Why hadn't she noticed it before? The bar where she always hung out was right across the street from the parking lot.

"Oh I almost forgot, I parked over here." Wiley started walking towards the parking lot near the bar. Justice turned her face away quickly. She thought she recognized three people sitting on a bench outside of the bar. It looked like Gregg, Rick, and Janet.

"Wiley!" Vance suddenly called. "Do you have those pictures of the storm we were talking about earlier? I haven't seen those yet.

" Oh yeah, there in my car come on."

Did she just hear right?

"Come on, let's go look at them. Wiley's a talented photographer."

Justice had no idea what to say, so she followed. She looked at the direction they were walking. They were going to have to walk across the street, and actually walk past the bar to get to the other parking lot. Past Gregg, Rick, and Janet.

Wiley slowed down, and waited for them. For that, Justice was grateful. Safety in numbers.

She walked in between Wiley, and Vance, and thought that maybe her old friends wouldn't see her.

If she was just a little bit shorter her plan would have worked, but she was tall, and although Wiley, and Vance were taller than her, they weren't quite tall enough.

"Look who it is." Justice heard the sneer, and recognized the voice before she had to turn.

"Thanks for ratting me out to Susan Janet."

Wiley, and Vance stopped, and stared at Justice's old friend.

"Gregg, Rick." Justice nodded.

Gregg gave a wave, he was wasted as usual, and Rick scowled. "Here's the foster brat."

"You're welcome. I thought you needed to get out of that perfect little home. You can thank me later."

Justice stopped, and glared at Janet with such a look, it made Janet flinch. Rick and Gregg squirmed.

"Well guess what? I still live there, and I'm not going anywhere. I'm done with you Janet. You can hang out with Gregg the dope, and Rick the toad all you want, but I'm out. "

"Did you just insult us?" Rick asked threateningly.

Justice gave a mock second to pretend she was thinking, and then replied "Yes, yes I did. Good job you caught on. Maybe you're not so dense after all."

Gregg laughed.

"He's worse don't worry." Justice pointed to Gregg "You're still one above Gregg."

Rick stood up quickly. "No sit back down, she's not worth your time." Janet told him, pushing him back down. "It's between Justice and me anyway."

"No it's not. You aren't worth my time. You're trailer trash." Even Justice couldn't believe what she had just said. That was one emotional blow to Janet, and Justice knew it. She had grown up in a trailer and had tried to pretend that she never had. It wasn't a nice one either, some of the trailers Justice saw were cute, but since Janet came from a mother who was into every drug she could afford, their home was a mess.

Vance's eyes bulged, and he whispered something to Wiley.

"What did you just say to me?" Janet got up and walked up to Justice. They were almost the exact same height, and weight. Justice wasn't intimidated though. She could tell that Janet had been drinking, and knew that she couldn't really do to much harm.

Justice gave her a hard shove, and pushed her away. "Get out of my face."

Janet was surprised and fell backwards. She got up quickly and said, "And you think you are better! At least I have a home! What happens when this foster family ditches you huh? Who are you gunna hang with then? Cuz you aren't coming back to us."

Wiley stepped forward then, and said "Well if that ever happens, she'll hang with me."

Vance Threw in, "And I doubt that will happen any time soon."

"Who are these people? They look like goodie-goodies." Gregg snickered.

Justice smiled. "This is Wiley, and Vance. My friend, and my new foster brother."

Janet looked a little surprised.

Vance only nodded. "Yeah, my family loves Justice. I don't think they'll be letting her go anytime soon."

"Well this was nice, but I have to go. Bye." Justice winked.

They quickly walked to Wiley's car. The parking lot was lit, and that was a good thing.

When they were out of ear shot Vance asked, "Did you want to get us killed or what Justice?"

"Relax, I knew they wouldn't do anything. Janet is a bully and bosses everybody around, but she's really a wuss when you stand up to her. I don't remember the last time I saw Gregg sober, and Rick is big, but he got gypped when they passed out brains."

"Still…" Vance went on.

"I had to let them have it. Janet almost ruined my life. Let me rephrase that: she was ruining my life. I'm glad I finally saw that before it was too late. "

"They're a tough crowed." Wiley whistled, as he pulled the pictures from his car.

"Yeah they are. Funny, I didn't see Ryan. I wonder where he was."

"Ryan? Did we want to see Ryan? Was he as creepy as the rest of them because…"

"No Vance, he's still one of my best friends. He hangs out with those guys but he's…different."

Wiley raised an eyebrow. "So that was your little posse. Wow."

"I know." Justice shrugged. "I guess I have you guys now though."

"You bet. You're stuck with us for life now." Wiley smiled. "Now look at these, aren't they great?" Vance and Justice admired Wiley's pictures for a few minutes. They were sitting inside of his car with the light on, and the doors locked.

"Wow the lightning is so powerful in this picture." Justice exclaimed. "It looks like it's about to hit something."

"I think it did." Wiley showed a picture of bits of trees flying up in the air.

After a time, Vance and Justice realized they should be getting home. Wiley drove them over to their car and, watched them get out. He clasped Vance's hand in a hand shake, and gave Justice a side hug.

"I'll see you guys at church tomorrow."
Vance climbed behind the wheel and started the car before Justice's seatbelt was on.
"Wow your anxious."
"Yeah, well with your little friends over there, the sooner we get out of here, the better." They sped away and got home in record time. Other than Janet and the other's disrupting their evening, they had, had a good time.

When they got inside the lights were out, and Vance announced that his parents usually went to bed early on Saturdays. His dad, since he was a pastor, had to be at the church really early and his mom would often go early too, and help out with nursery during the first service. They each headed to their rooms, so they could crash.

Jane and Bill had heard the door open, but they remained quiet. They didn't want to share the phone call that had just come from Susan. Jane's tears had finally stopped falling, but her pillow was still wet. Bill was awake, and didn't think that he would be sleeping much that night. Tomorrow was going to be a hard day. They wondered what they would even do when it was over.

Chapter Thirteen
The Unjust

This was it. She just had to make these people believe that Justice could be changed, and then they would adopt her. Justice would have a family, and live happily ever after. The family would know what to do with her, and she would be out of her hands. This had to work. Susan walked back to her office, and saw a couple sitting at her desk.

"Hello, I'm Susan Walker." Susan extended her hand to the man and the woman before sitting behind the desk.

"Hi, nice to meet you. My name's Charlie, and this is my wife Anna."

After the introductions were made, business was ready. Susan gave them the low down on Justice Clarks. Telling them everything they would possibly need to know. She whipped out the folder that contained everything, including all of the times that she snuck out.

"It says that she has snuck out well over a hundred times this year." Anna pointed out. She had a worried look on her face. "What would make her want to do that?"

"I guess it's when she's unhappy. Now the emergency foster family she's with at the moment, said that she's only snuck out once, and has promised not to do it again. So far she's kept her word."

"Okay." Anna nodded.

"I don't know why the sudden change, but I think it has something to do with the family. They really treat her as one of their own."

"Has she been around any other kids?" Charlie asked.

"This is her first time with foster siblings, but she seems to be doing well with them." Susan paused. "She should be fine."

"It says here, that she tends to have intense, sometimes violent fits of rage. What does this mean?"

"Oh, well she used to throw some temper-tantrums when she was little. She's outgrown that now."

Susan went on and told them many things. She told them about her rough upbringing and told them how Justice seemed to handle certain situations. She watered down some of the hard facts like Justice was found smoking once in a while, or that she probably wouldn't stay with them very long. She had to get someone to adopt her though. There just had to be somebody for her, and maybe they just needed a nudge. Susan thought she could provide that.

"Justice is really a nice girl when you get to know her. I'm sure you guys will bond quickly." If that wasn't lying through her teeth, Susan didn't know what was. It was all for a good cause though, it would be okay. She showed them pictures.

"Wow she's a pretty girl. You said she's sixteen? She could pass for older." Anna commented.

Susan nodded.

Charlie asked if they could talk privately for a moment, and Susan excused herself to make a call. She was going to call the psychologist back, and ask his opinion. The psychologist was all for it. He said that it would probably be the best thing for Justice, other than a mental hospital. Encouraged, Susan walked back into her office, and asked the couple if they were ready, or if they thought they would need more time to decide.

"Nope, I think we're ready." Charlie spoke, and Anna nodded.

"Okay, then what would you like to do?" Susan asked sitting at her desk, and sinking into her chair. This was the moment she had been waiting for, for years. It had to be time.

"We would really like to welcome her into our family, if she would be willing to come."

"Excellent!" Susan exclaimed. "Of course she will need to agree to it, but at the very least, I am authorized to place her with you guys, and out of the care of the emergency foster home she's in."

"Doesn't she have to agree to being moved?" Anna asked surprise flickering across her face.

"Well in most situations yes, but Justice has said that she wants a family, and I think she will be willing to give you guys a chance. After all, she has to give people a chance if she ever has hopes of being adopted. I'm afraid without my helpful little pushes, Miss Justice might be too nervous to take that first step."

Charlie and Anna both nodded in understanding.

"So I see you've fostered before." Susan thumbed through the files and paperwork that were scattered across her desk. "This should make the process go by much faster."

They worked out everything, and spent the rest of the day filling out paper work. Then it was time to call the Carters…Justice would be out of their hair by Monday morning…

Justice awoke to her alarm she had set the night before. Church started at 9:30. It was 7:30 but she wanted to make sure that she had enough time to get ready. She jumped into the shower, and then quickly dried off and got dressed. Her skirt, and shirt looked nice together, and she gave a little twirl. She blow dried her hair, and gave it a little bounce. Justice applied just a little bit of eye liner and mascara to make her eyes stand out more. Eye shadow made it look softer, so she added a little, and clear lip gloss completed her make-up.

She came down stairs and found that Vance was all ready, and he was just finishing breakfast.

"Good morning." She told him.

"Good morning." He replied. "Mom, and Dad are already gone. I think Valley went with them, she likes helping mom out with the nursery."

"Oh." Justice replied. She poured herself a bowl of cereal and sat next to Vance on the stool.

"Hey you fixed it."

"Yep. You really wrecked the finish though. I'll have to fix it sometime."

"Yeah I know." Justice smiled sheepishly.

"Oh I am not ready to get up today." Vance rubbed his face and whined a little more.

Justice could do with another couple hours of sleep too, but this was her first time in church. She was a little nervous.

They left ten minutes later and got to the church in less. It really was right across the street.

Vance and Justice found Wiley and Tanika sitting near the front, so they joined them. Justice looked around her, as they sang the first songs. They were a little different than the ones that they sang at youth group but they were still worship songs. Justice looked at the words on the overhead, and tried to sing along.

Wiley, and Vance were singing, Tanika was raising her hands, dancing along and singing. Talk about talented. Justice relaxed as they sang a few more songs. The worship leader had them all sit down, and then announced that the offering was about to come around. They passed the offering plates around and people dropped coins and paper money into the little golden trays. Justice only had a few bucks on her, but she dropped them into the plate as it came around. When offering was collected, a prayer was said to bless it and use it for God's name and glory. They all said 'amen' and were told to sit down. Now Bill came up to the pulpit and said a big "Good morning" with which the congregation replied "Good morning." Bill spoke a little about the worship that morning, and then read off some prayer requests. They prayed for all of the sick, and hurting in the church and praised the lord for those who were rejoicing. Bill then started the sermon. Something seemed different about Bill this morning though. He didn't look like happy Bill anymore...He actually looked kind of...sad.

"What's wrong with your dad?" Justice whispered to Vance.

"You noticed too? I don't have a clue. He's never been like this before, and whenever he has something on his mind, he let's the church know."

"Wow. It must be something pretty big."

"Yeah." Vance frowned. "Stay here, I'm going to find my mom real fast."

"Vance! Don't leave me here by myself..." Justice started.

"It's okay, Wiley and Tanika are here. All you have to do is sit and listen to my dad. No big deal."

Vance quickly left, and Wiley raised an eyebrow. Justice just shrugged.

What was Vance asking his mom about? What could possibly make Bill look that unhappy? He preached the sermon, and had

WHERE HOPE IS FOUND

a really energetic voice, but there was no gleam in his eye. She had never heard Bill preach before, but she had seen him talk. He was one of those people who were really passionate about what they were talking about. He had a way with words that made whatever he was talking about, always seem interesting. Justice knew how much he loved God, so where did the light go? She looked around at the congregation. Some people shifted in their seats a little, others didn't flinch. Justice couldn't tell if they knew something was wrong or not.

The sermon, was almost over and Vance still hadn't come back. Wiley leaned over and asked, "Where did Vance run off to?"

"He said he had to ask his mom something. " Justice thought for a moment. "I thought he said he would be right back." Justice started to feel that something was terribly wrong now. Where was Vance? Why was Bill so upset? She was getting anxious. What was going on? "Do you know where the nursery is?" She whispered over to Wiley.

"Uh huh. You know when you come in, that hallway on the left?"

Justice nodded.

"Well, you go down there, and turn right. It's the second door. There's a big NURSERY sign outside."

"Okay, I'm going to go find Vance."

"Are you sure? The service is almost over, and Vance may have had to make a pit stop or something. He'll be back."

But Justice wasn't convinced. "I don't know. I just want to see if he's there or not, I'll come back after."

"Okay." Wiley agreed. Justice snuck out of the pew, and down the long rows, to the back of the church. She exited quietly, and found the hallway. She turned right, and found the door. She wasn't really sure what made her do it, but she just stopped. She didn't want to go in. She peered through the little window on the door, to see if Jane and Vance were inside.

To her surprise they were. It was quiet in the room, so Justice could just make out some the words. Vance and Jane had their backs to Justice, which was probably a good thing, but it did muffle their voices a little. Jane was shaking a little as if she were…crying. Justice checked the hall, and listened for footsteps. Nothing echoed, so she pressed her ear to the door.

"…I just really don't know what to do Vance. How am I ever going to tell her?"

Valley maybe? But Valley was in the nursery too, right now she was playing catch with a toddler. Justice could just see her, out of the corner of the window.

"I really thought God sent her to us because he wanted us to adopt…but maybe not. Maybe not." Vance spun around and grabbed a tissue off of the little table that stood behind them. Justice ducked a little. He handed it to his mom, who wiped her eyes. So she was crying. Justice was trying to process what she was hearing. What was Jane talking about? Surely it wasn't about her…everything she said did seem to line up, but no. No. Susan understood about the incident. Bill had made sure of it. There was nothing wrong. This had nothing to do with her, nothing at all. Yet even as she tried to convince herself she heard the words uttered. "I guess Susan found a better family to adopt Justice." Justice's jaw dropped open in absolute horror at those words. Who was going to adopt her? Why? Nothing was wrong with the Carters and she knew that she could never live with anybody else. Susan knew. What was wrong? What had happened that the Carter's weren't telling her? Her mind flashed back to the look on Bill's face and Vance's disappearance during the service. They were all upset…over her. No. It couldn't be. Everything inside of Justice wanted to burst with anger, and hurt. How could the Carter's give her up so easily? Just like that? Was she wrong the whole time, when she thought they truly cared for her? Justice could feel a sob rising in her throat. She watched, unable to move as Vance comforted his mom, and Jane continued to weep. Valley has stopped playing catch now and was starting to cry as well. Now the whole family knew…but not her. They never told her. When were they going to tell her? What was their plan? To just say "Oh sorry, you can't live with us anymore, you're being adopted, by some freaky family you don't know?" Justice couldn't breath. She moved away from the door and slumped against the wall. She put her hands on her knees, and could feel them trembling. What was she going to do? The Carter's were going to give her up and Justice knew, from the depths of her heart, that she couldn't live with another family. This was it. She was burned out completely. The candle had been dimming after a few years, but now the light was out, and the wick was in ashes. She was ruined. Justice felt hot tears pour over her red cheeks. She heard footsteps coming. Probably one of the moms coming to pick up her kid, but Justice couldn't move. She tried to at least muffle the sobs that seemed to be coming out in hiccups. It hardly helped. She had tried to so hard. She wanted them to love her; she wanted Susan to be proud. It was all to no avail. Once again her heart was broken.

Justice couldn't stop the tears from rolling. The footsteps were closer, and she heard them stop directly in front of her. She couldn't look. Up.

"Here you are, so did you find…" Wiley's voice trailed off, as he saw Justice crying. "Justice…Are you okay?"

Justice tried to find some words. Nothing seemed to form in her dry mouth. There was nothing she could say to express how she felt at this moment. The sobs were getting worse and Justice was starting to hyperventilate. Time to get going, before she made a scene. Like she hadn't already. With the rest of her weakened strength she could muster, she sprinted past Wiley, down the hall, around the corner and out of the Church. She didn't hear Wiley call after her, and she didn't see Jane open the nursery door, to see what the noise was about. She just kept running. She had no idea what she was doing or where she was going to go. She was just running away from the pain. There was no way she was going to call Susan. Her old friends would never see her again, after the things she had said to them. Not that she would really want to see them anymore anyway. She sprinted and jogged, until she felt like her legs would collapse and her heart would burst. She looked around, and for the first time realized that she was at a park. She flopped down on a bench and let the tears that had been bottled up for years flow. She cried and cried, unable to stop. The Carter's were abandoning her. She was going to be sent away. Adopted yes, but sent away. Who knew what the family she was going to be placed with was like? Justice was sure she had never met them before, so there was no way in the world they knew who she was. Were they just some family desperate to adopt a kid? What would they do to her? She had heard stories of some of the awful homes orphans were placed in. Of course the social workers and agencies always tried to prevent that sort of stuff from happening, but sometimes they failed. Even if they ended up being the nicest family in the world, Justice knew that she would never love them the way she had grown to love the Carter's in just one week. One week, and her life had been forever altered. Against her will she had begun to believe that maybe she had a home. Now she knew how right she was about letting her heart's guard down. Never let it down. She hit the bench with her fist and was glad that the park was abandoned. She was really making a scene. She didn't care though. Nothing mattered anymore. Justice remembered the last time she had felt this intense mix of pain, and rage. It was when the Johnson's car crashed. Justice closed her eyes, and remembered the terrible day.

"We won't be gone long honey, don't worry. We just want to go out on a date tonight. It's our anniversary." The Johnson's smiled at each other, and Justice knew that it was okay. She was seven. She knew who her neighbors were, and could call them in case of an emergency. The Johnson's wouldn't be gone long, and she knew that the sitter would be a good one. Justice kissed them goodbye, and watched them walk out the door. She went upstairs to play with her toys while the sitter cooked some macaroni and cheese for dinner. It was her favorite. The time past slowly, and Justice ate her dinner, cleaned up her toys, and got in the bath. All of the things the Johnsons wanted her to do. After her bath, the sitter announced that it was bed time. Justice usually had someone read her a story, but she would let it slide for tonight. She didn't want to go to sleep until they got home. She waited and waited, fighting to stay awake. Finally, she gave in and went to sleep. She was startled awake about midnight, and couldn't understand why the sitter woke her up so late. Then she announced that they were going to the hospital, to see the Johnson's. Justice didn't understand why. The sitter refused to say anything the whole ride over. When they got to the hospital, they waited in an uncomfortable waiting room for what seemed forever. Finally a doctor came out, his face grim. "I'm sorry; we were unable to save the Johnson's."

Justice hadn't understood, what that meant, so she asked the sitter. "I'm sorry Justice, the Johnson's died in a car accident." The world came crashing down, and everything was confused after that...so many new faces and homes. Nothing was ever the same...But Justice thought it was about to get better. Maybe not. The Johnson's were gone, and now the Carter's. Justice had finally stopped crying, and her head felt as if someone was banging it with a hammer. She was at the park, doing nothing. She was by herself, and the Carter's didn't know where she went. She simply left them. What now? What now? The question kept turning around in her head and she couldn't come up with an answer. She didn't want to run, and she didn't want to hide. All the drugs and alcohol in the world would never take away this pain. It would numb it for a while, but then it would be back and there would be more of it. The tears jumped back into her eyes, at the thought of her helplessness. She had no home, no money and no life. She was sitting here at a park, and nobody knew where she was. She truly was alone in the world. The many conversations she had with the Carter's came back to her. "Jesus loves you."

"He can take anything bad and use it for good."

"If you don't believe in God, then what do you believe in?" That made her laugh. She had responded "Fate" and "luck." Well suddenly her fate was looking pretty bleak, and her luck seemed to have run out. Not that she had, had a ton to begin with. So that left God. Justice never really thought about God too much. He was a crutch for those who needed one. Yes her life might be hard, but she was proud. She didn't need anybody's help. No help from parents, siblings or friends. She never thought she needed God's. Jane said that he was always there with her and that he would never leave her side. She was feeling so abandoned, even that thought sounded comforting. The thought that God was there...Still something inside of her wouldn't let go. How could she believe in a God who had looked past all of her pain? How did God stand by and watch a mother beat her four-year-old daughter? "Why God, if you're so real, kind and loving... Why did you do this to me? Why do you hate me so much?" Justice let out a harsh whisper. Did God sit up there and move people around like chess game? Was she on the losing side? What had she done? Justice sat there, very still. Going through her options. It was nearing evening, and Justice realized that she had been gone for several hours. The Carter's were probably looking for her…but suddenly she didn't want to be found. She didn't want to see them again. She stood up from the bench determined not to be found. Where would she go? Justice thought for a moment. Maybe she would just wander around for a while. She did that sometimes. When she was unhappy she would just walk around, and look at different things. Different buildings and trees, and whatever else seemed to be around. She walked aimlessly. Away from the park, and just kept walking on the side walk. She went straight sometimes, and other times she would turn a corner. She was thirsty, so she stopped at a little super market and used some change to buy herself a drink. Then she left and walked on. The day had turned to evening and now it was falling to night. Justice knew it could be dangerous walking around, but she wasn't worried. She wasn't worth a thing. It didn't matter what happened to her anymore. Justice stared at the side walk as she walked. She wasn't really taking in her surroundings anymore. Finally she looked up, and a smile twitched her lips. A pretty neighborhood opened up in front of her. The houses were beautiful, most of them must have been multi-million dollar homes. Justice decided to walk in there and look around. It was getting really dark now, and the sun was gone. It was a full moon though, and Justice was grateful that it lit things up. She looked at the houses. Some of them still had lights on, and the curtains were open. Probably to show everybody how wealthy they were. She saw one house that made her stop and catch her breath. It wasn't actually the house that has caused her to stop, it was the family crowded around the table for dinner. It looked like a big family gathering. She saw several older couples, probably grandparents and saw other adults and children sitting around the table. Aunts and uncles, and cousins. Justice let a few tears fall. They were all so happy. They lived in a wonderful house and ate such wonderful food. The window was open, and she could smell chicken, and potatoes wafting outside. They must have an incredible feast inside. They were all together. Parents were hugging and scolding their children for running in the house, while others were scooping food onto their plates. A baby sat contentedly swinging his little legs, while his grandma held him. The family was chatting and trading stories about the day. The house glowed with a warmth that Justice burned to feel. She had felt it with the Carter's. Just watching this family made her think about them. They didn't live in the biggest house, and their family wasn't huge, but they had loved Justice as much as their own kids. They gave her everything they had to offer. Even when she ran off that one night. After all of the rude things she had said to them, and the disrespect she had shown, they still loved her.

Her eyes burned with new tears. How could this happen? Everything was lining up perfectly. Things were finally going in the right direction. In one week her hopes could be renewed and dashed away. In One single week. It felt so unjust. She turned her eyes away from the sight, and decided to look somewhere to spend the night.

She ended up walking all the way back to the little park she had started at. It took a while, but she was happy just to find a place to sit. Her legs felt as if they would just fall off. Her stomach growled since she her last meal was breakfast, but she would brave hunger for the night. As long as she could sleep. So she found her bench and sat quietly down. Justice curled up and closed her eyes. She was asleep in minutes.

Chapter Fourteen
The Search

 Justice hadn't come home, and the Carter's were worried sick. No one had seen her since church. When Jane opened the nursery door, all she had seen was a dumbstruck Wiley. She had heard retreating footsteps that she now knew belonged to Justice. Wiley said that Justice was upset about something and that she went to go find Vance. Putting it all together, they realized that Justice found out about the adoption before any of them had the chance to tell her. Jane could only imagine the pain she was going through. Bill was out searching for her, and Vance had taken his car out too. Jane raked her nervous hands through her hair. So far Justice couldn't be found and she was supposed to be transferred the next morning. Everything was a complete mess. Nothing seemed to have gone right. Jane finally broke down and started crying. She walked over to the couch and put her head in her hands. She was glad that she had decided to send Valley upstairs to bed. Valley had been very worried about Justice, but Jane didn't want her to have to deal with everything at the moment. She couldn't let Valley have a break down when she was in the middle of one herself.
 "God, I could really use some help about now." She prayed.

"I have no idea what to do. Please, watch over Justice. Wherever she is." Jane calmed down a little then. She knew what she had to do. She had to call Susan. In the back of her head, she felt a warning. Justice was supposed to be in a mental home right now. What exactly made Susan consider that? Was It just the running away, or was it something else? The need to find Justice quickly kept her heart pounding, and the adrenalin rushing. What was Justice up to? She dialed Susan's number and waited impatiently for it to ring. She was in the middle of making an earnest message for Susan to call her as soon as possible when she picked up.

"Hello? Jane Carter?"

Jane caught her breath before she answered, "Oh Susan I'm glad you picked up. Justice is gone, she's missing. She ran away." Jane couldn't seem to get everything she needed to say out. "I think, I think she found out about being switched to a different foster home. Before we could tell her that is, and now she's just gone. We haven't seen her since church…"

"Wait slow down Jane." Susan said calmly. "You said you haven't seen her since church? So she's been gone all day?"

"Yes! I have no idea where else to look. I would have called you sooner but we've barely been home all day. At first I just thought she needed some time to herself, and that she would be back for lunch, but when that didn't happen we got worried. We only got back a couple hours ago and I was afraid to make any calls, in case she called…"

"Okay, Justice runs away a lot. It's not unlike her to not come home at night." Susan paused. "However, this is a different situation. She really liked you guys. I didn't see this one coming." Susan sounded so uncertain which really scared Jane, because she usually knew all about Justice, and would predict her intentions. Now she was empty. Justice really had them this time.

The words. *"I'm going to kill myself..."* Floated back to Susan's memory. She gasped.

"What is it?" Jane demanded.

"Oh my gosh, we need to find her soon!"

"What Susan, what?" Jane screamed into the phone.

"Before I called you guys to pick her up, Justice told me that she was going to kill herself..."

"That's why you were going to send her to the...?"

"Part of it yes. She was out of control, and when she announced that...I believed her more than ever."

"Oh, oh no. We have to hurry. I'll call Bill and tell him." Jane paused. "Susan we can't let anything happen to her." Jan cried into the phone. "I love her."

"I know. So do I." Jane thought she heard Susan's voice crack.

"I'll start looking around for her. I don't know if she would be around here, but she knows the place well. I'll get down to the agency right away." Jane realized then that she had called Susan at her house, and it was the middle of the night. Funny how she didn't even check the time. Most of the time she would never imagine calling somebody this late at night. This was different though. Justice was her daughter, maybe only until tomorrow...but she was today, and nothing was going to keep her from getting her back.

They hung up determined, and Jane called Bill on his cell phone with the frantic message. Bill called Vance and spread the news. They doubled their efforts, and Vance called his friends to help with the search.

Susan hung up and let the tears wash over her. After all these years with Justice... The girl was a pain that was true. There were definitely times when Susan just wanted to send her away and be done with it. She cared about her though; she knew that now, more than any time in her life. She had spent her life trying to find the girl a home. A good home at that. By getting a family to adopt her, she thought she was doing Justice a favor. However, everything she did seemed to be a mistake. In all the times she had tried to win, Susan couldn't help the fact that she had failed. She had failed Justice. She had failed herself and ruined it for all who may have been able to love Justice. Nobody got anything now. If Justice committed suicide, Susan knew that she would never be able to forgive herself. Everything in the world had to be done to stop Justice from making the biggest mistake in her life. Susan grabbed her car keys and slammed the door to her apartment.

Justice awoke with a start. The sun was shining brightly and fell between the limbs of the tree, which shaded her. She sat up, and quickly glanced around. A lady with a dog jogged by on a little path that surrounded the park. She didn't seem to be paying much attention though. The park was pretty empty. Justice couldn't believe it. She had stayed out all night. The Carter's had never found her. Then an awful thought struck her...maybe the Carter's never looked for her in the first place. It was an awful thing to think about, but she had to consider it. She could make it on her own. She'd done it before. Lasted three days outside and never complained once. That was before all of this happened though. The possibilities swirled around in her head like an endless merry-go-round, but she didn't really have the heart to try and figure one out. If she had somewhere else to go, maybe she would take that option, but there was no way that she would be adopted by some other family. No way at all. She couldn't let it happen. In fact, she would rather die than be placed with a family other than the Carter's. How could she make Susan understand? Justice thought back to all of the times she had tried to manipulate her. It never really worked. She sighed, trying to come up with a plan. Nothing would come to mind. Susan was as stubborn as a cat, and would never agree to let Justice stay with the Carter's. Never. With that mindset, Justice realized that her life looked really dark in the future. There was no possible escape and if there was no escape than she would much rather die. Dark thoughts started to crowd her head. Reluctantly at first, she listened to them. The voice told her she was worthless, nobody cared about her and the other family would be horrible. To live would cause unnecessary torture. Yes, it was much better to die, and be done with it. But how would she die? What would she do? Was she brave enough to go out with her plan? Justice shivered at the thought. She looked around her, and something caught her attention. Way on the other side of the park and beyond the trees, Justice saw something glitter. She squinted, got up and headed towards the trees. A few minutes later she was standing beneath the trees. The trees opened up into a little trail and Justice could see a shimmering lake at the end. Small boats sailed off in the distance. Justice saw a few people fishing. It was pretty early out, but Justice could imagine what the lake would look like by lunch time. There was a little beach that had warm golden sand, and Justice walked to the waters edge, and stuck her hand in it. It was warm, and clear. She saw one of the men start too real in his fishing line, and haul a big fish onto the boat. Deciding to check out the peer, she headed over to it and walked to the end. The peer extended a little ways, and Justice sat on the edge of it and let her legs dangle. They didn't quite reach the water, but she could tell that it was pretty deep. The water was calm and Justice could see her reflection in it. An Idea had already popped into her head, but no matter how hard she tried, she couldn't push it away. She would come back to this pretty place at night, and take a swim. Maybe she would decide to stay in the water for ever. She would never have to deal with Susan, the Carter's, or anybody ever again. She would just die, and it would be a comforting sleep that she would never wake from. Tears trickled down her face, and into the water. *Face it Justice, this is just the way it has to end…your life won't get any better. You tried it remember? You gave the Carter's a shot and they let you down. They are going to give you away, and you'll never see them again. Do you want to spend the rest of your life with a family you've never me? O do you want to do the smart thing and get rid of the pain once and for all? Wouldn't ending this nightmare be the best thing for you?* She began to think. *Maybe it would be the best thing for me. I did give it a chance, and they did fail me. I've always said that my life won't get any better, so why don't I just end it? Only I can end my suffering.*

Justice could feel the struggle within herself. While one side told her to jump, the other side kept saying, *No Justice don't throw it all away. You don't know what will happen, anything is possible. The Carter's love you, and they would never do anything to hurt you. They are looking for you right now. Don't do it, don't do it, don't do it!*

There was a point there too. She didn't know what would happen. Nobody could know how this would work out in the end. A miracle could happen, and she could get to stay with the Carter's after all. Plus what happened after death? Where would she go? According to Bill and Jane, if she died then she would be going to hell because she didn't believe in God. Then again, since she didn't believe in God, there was really no reason to fear…right? The other voice persisted, and she felt a strong desire to die, but not before she wrote one last letter to the carters…

The cars were gone and Justice knew that the Carter's weren't home. They may have been looking for her or even throwing a party. Who knew? It didn't matter though, because she was only going to leave a note on the door and leave. She wanted to make sure the Carter's got it. She slipped the note under the screen of their front door and made sure that it couldn't blow away. Then she turned and walked back down the driveway. She stopped at the end and glanced back. It was the last time she would ever look upon this house. The house that she had wanted so badly to be her home. Yet it could never be, so it was better to just escape the pain and misery that seemed to follow her every step. She smiled fondly at the place, and whispered. "Bye Carters." Then she ran down the street, determined to never look back and never be found.

"Oh Jane. I have no idea where she could be. We've looked everywhere! I've called everybody at church and told them to be on the look out for her. Most of them volunteered to help and are searching the area just as we are. The prayer team has been alerted, and they are gathering as we speak, to pray for us and Justice."

"I know." Jane wiped her eyes. "Everybody is really pitching in to help. It's wonderful… I just wish Justice knew how many people were looking for her! She would never be able to say she wasn't loved again."

"We have to find her. Justice is a smart girl, she would

never...?" But even as he said it, he felt that she was capable of suicide. Bill was blinking back tears and trying very hard to keep his head. This was a time for thinking rationally and keeping a clear head. He would be no help to Justice if he lost it.

"Bill, we have to find her. There's no other option, we have to."

"I know, I agree. We *will* find her."

As Vance pulled up to the driveway he hoped, and prayed with all his heart that Justice was inside making a sandwich. That she had decided to crash at one of her old friend's places and decided to return for food. That's why he would come home, if he ever ran away. What would a teen girl come home to get? Vance tried to imagine for a moment, as he unlocked the door, and stepped inside. The word *clothes* popped into his brain, and he ran up the stairs and headed to Justice's room. He was still in shock that Justice had been put into that room. It had been Vanessa's and he remembered when his mom, and her painted it together. Vanessa was really into pink. His mom had decided to put Justice in Vanessa's old room, when Valley refused to share her own. His mom, not wanting to cause more problems, gave in. He opened the door and peered inside. Nothing had changed. The bed was still made and Justice's back pack was in the corner. All of her clothes were still placed neatly in their drawers and nothing had been touched. It was obvious: Justice had never come home. Where would she go? It wasn't like she had a ton of money, and staying with her old friends wasn't a big option was it? The thought was at least a good place to start, maybe she had decided to go back to her old ways. It seemed so unlikely, especially after the fight she had, had the other day, but anything was possible with Justice. He walked back down the stairs, and decided to check the rest of the house first. He looked in all of the bed rooms just in case. He yelled her name, and looked inside the garage, but Justice could not be found. Finally he went back outside and locked the door behind him. He stepped off of the porch, and his shoe crumpled something. A piece of paper littered the ground and Vance muttered,

"Man I hate when people litter." He picked the piece of paper up between his fingers and glanced at it quickly. He opened the lid to the trash can and threw it inside. As it fell, it flipped over and Vance saw *Carters* and his heart stopped. "Oh no!" The paper fell under a heavy trash bag and he groaned. "Oh great!" Without another thought he plunged his arm into the giant bin and fished around for the piece of paper. He grimaced as his fingers brushed against some very slimy objects. "This better be an important letter." Vance grumbled. After finding all sorts of disgusting things, he finally pulled out the piece of paper, now wet with who-knows-what. It was folded in half and he quickly opened it, and read the note:

Dear Bill, Jane, Vance and Valley,
I want you guys to know how much I love you.
You guys have been the best family that I have ever Lived with! I know that you can't keep me forever though, and I wish with all my heart that there was another way to stay.
I have to admit that when I first came to this family, I didn't plan to give you guys a chance, but you sure changed my mind...
So much that I can never live in another home again. I never want to be away from you guys. But I know that isn't realistic. So I want to say goodbye for good. I don't think anybody will really care that much.
Susan will be much happier, everybody else will have one last Justice to worry about and you guys won't have to deal with me Ever again... Nobody else will ever have to let me down.

I love you guys forever and thank you for the kindness that You have shown me.

Justice Clarks

Vance gasped. This was too horrible. Justice was going to commit suicide! Vance grabbed his head, and tried to breath normally. "Easy Vance, just breath." He finally caught his breath and realized "Okay, she must have come home earlier today, maybe only moments before I pulled up. She can't be dead yet." He checked his watch and saw the time. He decided to call his parents on their cell phone first.

The phone rang, and Jane answered it eagerly. "Hello, any sign?"

'Hi mom, it's Vance." Her son replied.

"Hi Hun, how are you doing, any word?" The questions were fast, but if Vance noticed he made no comment.

"Mom, I don't know how to say this."

"Say what?" Jane demanded. Her nerves were completely shot and she couldn't help snapping.

"Well, Justice left a note…"

"What note!" Jane screamed so loud that Bill jumped, and swerved the car a little.

"Jane calm down, I don't want to crash." Bill said calmly.

Jane nodded and asked more softly. "What did it say Vance?"

"Mom…Uh…" Vance stuttered a little. "Mom it said she was going to kill herself!"

Jane gave a cry of alarm and then said, "Oh that's what I was afraid of!"

"Here I'll read the note…" Vance read the note allowed, and tried to keep his voice steady but it still shook a little. It was the most painful thing that he was ever forced to read. When he

finished he exclaimed, "I just found it a minute ago. There still could be time…"
"I know." Jane cut in. "There has to be."
Vance nodded to himself. "I'll keep looking."
"And so will we." Jane promised. "I love you Vance okay?"
"I love you too, mom." Jane hung up, after the phone went dead and struggled from going insane. She doubted that Justice had any clue what kind of emotional stress she was putting on them. "How could she do this to everybody?" she asked allowed. Bill reached over and grabbed her hand. Jane squeezed it hard.

Vance knew it was a long shot but he had to try. He parked in the parking space that belonged to the bar and hopped out. He ran inside and searched the crowed for a familiar face. He found Janet, her boyfriend and Gregg. Justice wasn't kidding when she said this was their home-away-from-home. There was some other guy sitting with them too, but he didn't know who it was. "Guys I need your help," he said as soon as he was in talking distance, which was pretty much across the room. It was more like a yell but he was desperate. When the group ignored him, Vance roared, "Hey Janet, I'm talking to you."
Janet spun around and her over eye-shadowed eyes rolled at him. "What do you want, preppy?"
"I want to know where Justice is. Tell me."
"I haven't seen her since she was here the other night making a scene. Are you kidding me? We would never let her back in, after all the things she said to me. Right guys?" Gregg and Rick shook their heads, and the guy sitting next to Gregg just rolled his eyes.
"You guys are positive? This is a life-or-death situation! Justice might be in huge trouble!"
"Yeah well the girl is trouble what do ya expect?" Janet

inhaled her cigarette and breathed out smoke.

"She is going to kill herself!" Vance exclaimed. "I have to find her before its too late."

Gregg, and the other guy looked up at that and seemed a little stunned, but Janet only snickered. "Let her. Who needs her anyway?"

Vance was so close to hitting her right then and there that he had to take a step back. "She's my sister and I care."

"Your foster sis actually, and she ran away preacher boy...obviously she can't stand your little family anyway. Just get used to rejection okay hun?"

Vance was the closest that he had ever been to swearing, but he bit his tongue. "How can you be so heartless?" The last statement flew from his lips and he turned and stormed out of the door. He walked to his car, and unlocked it.

Vance was about to get in when he heard, "Wait!" He spun around, and saw the other guy from the table. The one he had never seen before.

"I'm Ryan, a friend of Justice's. You said she's going to kill herself? How do you know?"

Vance nodded. "Okay gets in, you can help me look for her and I'll explain on the way."

So Ryan hopped in and Vance started the car. He was giving a total stranger that he had found in a bar, a ride. It might have seemed absurd in most cases, but this one was justified.

The day dragged on and on. The police were alerted and the whole town seemed to be looking for an orphan girl named Justice Clarks. So why couldn't she be found? Jane had cried all of the tears she had and no more could fall. The only time she had cried like this was when Vanessa died. Even then, she remained strong for her family and would only cry in private.

How was Justice getting away? How could they have possibly missed her? Janet glanced in the back seat. Valley was fast asleep, and snoring slightly. Bill had offered to take Valley and her home, but they had both wanted to keep looking. Valley had insisted that she wasn't tired but it seemed that sleep had won. Valley had been through the same amount as both of them the past few days, so it was no surprise that she was exhausted. Jane thought about Valley. What would happen if Justice was found dead? Would Valley have a complete break-down just as she had with Vanessa? This was so hard on all of them. Didn't Justice know that she wasn't only hurting herself but that she was hurting everybody? She was killing the Carter's as well. Jane could feel her heart dying as each hour ticked by, with no sign of the girl. It was getting dark out and pretty soon it would be hard to see.

"Bill, the sun's almost gone."

"I know Jane. I know." Bill said softly.

Jane closed her eyes and prayed. "Father, you know where Justice is right at this moment. Oh lord we can't bear to see her go. Please show us where she is. I know we let you down when we agreed to give her away to the other family, but oh lord, if you would just give us a second chance, I promise that we would fight for custody of her. We would love her as one of our own." Jane took a breath. "We already love her as one of our own. My heart is breaking for her. You know that she doesn't know you yet and that if she ended her life, she would be separated from you forever. Please, be there for her now. Reveal yourself to her and save her before it's too late." Jane opened her eyes and searched the endless string of cars around her. Justice wasn't in one. She wasn't anywhere. In that one moment, Jane was sure that she had lost her second little girl.

It was dark now and nobody was out on the lake tonight. Justice sat on the peer and let her feet dangle. She had already felt the water and noticed the chill it now had to it. She took a deep breath and realized what she was about to do.

She was going to end her life in just a few moments. What would it be like? Would she fall asleep from lack of oxygen or would she struggle for several minutes before losing consciousness? She shuddered at the thought. Maybe she shouldn't think about it. The weather was changing and it was getting colder out. Justice could hear thunder starting to rumble. There was going to be a storm tonight. It started to rain, little drizzles at first that gradually turned to large rain drops pouring from the sky. The thunder was getting louder and the rain drops heavier. Lightning flashed across the sky and thunder followed with a thunderous clap. It was close. She sat, letting the rain pelt her with its cold water and seeing the lake ripple with the drops that fell from the sky. She was soaked and her hair was matted to her face. Yet she didn't move. Memories, which had long ago been forgotten, burned across her brain. She was remembering, even though she had tried to hide them all of these years. She remembered saying goodbye to her brother Sam. It was hard, and she never knew that she wouldn't see him again. Her mom had taken her that day and locked her in a dark closet. Now Justice knew it was to keep her from running away with her brother. Her mom had forgotten her and her dad had left. She was pretty much dead in their eyes. She was stuck in that closet for days. Her parents never came back for her. She was alone and hungry. Why had they forgotten her? What did she do wrong? Justice closed her eyes, and cried. All the nightmares, weren't only nightmares. They were her past. It was time to reflect upon her life, whether she wanted to or not. She thought back to all she could remember. She was born into a poor family that was dirty and smelled. She would never forget the awful smell of that place. She had many siblings, but they were all taken away from her neglective parents. She didn't even know all of her siblings because she was the youngest one. She did have a good big brother though and he was only two years older than she. Justice loved Sam. When the agency came to pick him up, she did want to go with him. She had actually begged to go with them, but the social worker had said that he couldn't take her with him this time. It was a hard concept for a four-year-old to learn. She was losing her brother. When the rest of the year didn't improve, the agency finally sent a social worker to get her out and place her in foster care. But not before, she had suffered a great amount. Her mother beat her constantly, and she was often neglected. Her father acted like she didn't even exists, and she barely knew he existed, except for when he came home drunk to beat his wife. She always hid during that period and was spared his wrath. Her mom believed in cruel and unusual punishments so when she was bad, she was put into that dreaded closet. Justice would have rather been beaten then be placed in there. Starvation was another good one, her mother liked to use. Home was not a safe place, but neither was their neighborhood. She was afraid to go outside, because their were bad people out there. She pretty much believed that the whole world was bad. One day a social worker found her in the closet and took her to the agency. It was the first time she had ever met Susan. When she came in, Susan took pity on her and spent a lot of time with her. She stayed with Justice when they were finding foster homes. Susan was nice to her and never shouted or hit Justice. She always made sure she was fed and warm. Susan asked her a lot of questions about her home, but she found that she couldn't really remember what her home was like. She told her about her brother Sam and how her house smelled bad. She would mention her mother and father and announced that they were mean, but she couldn't remember little details like theirs names, or where she lived. Susan asked her if she had grandparents or aunts and uncles, but Justice didn't even know what those were. She had never been to pre-school and never played with other kids her own age. Susan seemed surprised. Now she knew what an awful life she had. The first family she was placed with kept her for three years. But when they died she was placed back into foster care again. Susan was there for her but Justice was upset. She didn't want to be back at the agency. Susan, assured her, that they would find another loving family for her, but she didn't want another one. She wanted the Johnsons. They had loved her and that love had over-ruled any bad memories she had about parents. But when they died, the memories came flooding back. True to her word, Susan did find other families for her to stay in. However Justice didn't like them and they didn't seem to like her too much. They kept sending her back to the agency every few weeks. She couldn't understand why. Susan would place her with another family a week later, and her head would spin with all of the new faces and houses. Things just went down hill from there. By the time she reached twelve she had become who she was now. Justice smirked and a sad smile twitched her lips. There came a day when she realized the real reason the foster families had sent her away. Most of them never want to, but her mother wasn't cooperating and wouldn't sign adoption papers. She remembered the day that all changed…

Susan told her that her mother had died. She didn't tell her how she died, but Justice had found the paper that explained the details in a drawer in Susan's office. Justice was learning to read better in the public school she attended and so she read the information without too much trouble. She was a little disgusted with the way it happened, but not all that surprised. The worst thing was that she was glad that her mother had died. Now somebody could adopt her and it wouldn't matter if her mom wouldn't sign the right papers. She was dead. It seemed her mom was at home, and drugged up so much, that she probably never knew what was really happening. Her father came home and was as drunk as could be. He beat his wife to death and then ended up in prison for it. To this day, he was locked up on charges of murder.

The dark memories lasted a time and Justice just let herself remember. She was shaken back to reality when a huge thunder clap made her jump. The rain was pouring hard, while lightning flashed and thunder roared. The water was getting a little restless from all of the wind and the once peaceful lake had turned into a war zone between natures. It was time.

Justice jumped off the peer, and into the cold water.

Wiley Taylor, hadn't known a storm was coming. He usually did, but this seemed to be a freak of nature. He quickly ran out the door, with camera in hand. There was a park a few miles away from the church with a big lake. It would make a great picture. He ran to his car and jumped in. The wind was blowing the rain in his face as he hurriedly slammed the door shut. He had his cell phone in case Vance called with anymore news about Justice. He had prayed for her a million times and couldn't stop worrying. Maybe this would take his mind off of it for a few moments. As he rushed down there, hoping the storm would last so he could snap a good picture, Wiley thought about Justice's letter. Vance called him and read it over the phone. Why would she want to kill herself? He knew that she must have had a rough life, but how could she think suicide was the answer? It was the last thing he would do if he was in a terrible situation. He knew however, that she wasn't a Christian. His faith would be the thing that kept him going but take that away, as well as his family and what did he have? Nothing. That's why Justice was going to end her life. Because she didn't see all that she really had. If he could only find her and tell her that, it would be the best thing he could ever do for her. With a sad sigh, he realized that he had, had a chance to tell her about Christ's love and he didn't take it. He didn't want to offend her because she was new to the whole church idea, and he thought it was the *best* thing at the time. Now he knew with a troubled heart, that he had really kept the *best* thing from her. "If you would just let me find her Lord, I wouldn't let you down." Wiley breathed a prayer. He drove on, and the rain kept pouring. The storm wasn't about to let up. It still had a purpose to fulfill and it kept rumbling on. He pulled into the park and parked. As he hopped out, he pulled the hood of his sweatshirt over his head. In his haste to make it, he had forgotten his rain jacket. The lake was getting restless and there were waves rolling around the little beach that surrounded it. He walked over to the peer and the lightning flashed, illuminating a figure sitting with legs dangling in the water. His heart raced. What was he doing out in a storm like this? Was he homeless? He snapped a picture of the lonely person and decided he could write a newspaper article about it sometime. Maybe people would start to feel a little compassion for people without homes. He started to walk up to the figure, when it stood up and jumped into the lake! "Hey!" Wiley yelled, and sprinted across the peer. He glanced into the water and the lightning flashed again, revealing dark hair that swirled in the water. His heart leapt in his mouth and he nearly choked. The figure was slowly sinking to the bottom of the deep water and wasn't fighting to get back up. It looked like suicide. Wiley whipped off his sweatshirt and slipped out of his shoes. Without really knowing what he was doing, he dove into the lake, prepared to save this drowning person. His hands groped blindly around for the person and he desperately tried to open his eyes to see. The lake water stung, but he was determined. Black hair swept across his face and in his mouth. He pushed it away, but then realized what it was. He found the person's head and finally found the arm, which he grabbed and tried to drag back up to the surface. The person turned around under water and fought. Wiley's heart stopped beating and he gasped. Unfortunately his lungs filled with water and he started choking. Justice's eyes stared back at him and she moved out of his reach. Wiley had no choice; he had to get more air. He swam towards the surface and coughed out the remaining water in his lungs. Justice was down there! She was trying to drown herself and he couldn't let that happen. He dove back down, and searched for her. The water was getting really murky from the waves dragging up all the dirt and sand in the bottom. It was hard to see. He wanted to yell for her, but knew it wasn't an option. Wiley came back to the top and searched the surface. The lightning flashed and illuminated the lake. There! He found her. She was floating on top of the water, going half under and getting spat back out. *Thank you God, for lightning!* Wiley let out a quick prayer, and swam to Justice. The water was cold and he could feel it seeping into his bones, causing to him to become more tired. But he swam, determined not to let the water win. "God give me the strength to go on." He prayed out loud.

Justice's body was being pulled further and further out to the middle of the lake and Wiley knew he needed to swim faster, to reach her in time. Minutes ticked by and he still swam. Justice had been in the cold water for about ten minutes now, and wasn't fighting to make it back. She was trying to die. It was dark and he couldn't see very much. He knew that he was swimming in the right direction, but he couldn't seem to find her. He felt something brush against him and he reached out for it. It felt like hair. The lightning flashed again, and Justice was right beside him. It made him jump a little, but he was glad that he had found her.

"Justice!" He yelled at her. "Justice Can you hear me?" She was floating limply, and wasn't responding. "Oh no." Wiley felt panicked, but he knew he had to get her back to the peer. He slipped his arm around her waist, determined to drag her back to land. But the peer seemed like it was further away then he remembered and he didn't know if he would have the strength to swim both of them back. He realized that it would be hard to get Justice back on the peer too. The beach appeared closer, so he decided to try that way. He swam with one arm and kicked his legs hard. He was glad for those summer swimming lessons his mother had insisted on when he was a child. They were moving forward and although it was hard, he felt that he could make it. He looked back every once in a while, to make sure Justice's head was above the water. He had to get her to land fast. He couldn't tell if she was breathing or not. However, it wouldn't have been any better if she was awake, because she would be fighting him to stay in the water. He swam and swam. The beach appeared before him. A wave pushed him the last little distance to shore and they rolled against it roughly. Wiley lost hold of Justice for a moment when they landed, but he saw that she was only a few feet away from him. He crawled over, and raised her head. She didn't move. "Justice!" He yelled. She didn't make a sound, so Wiley shook her. The shaking did the trick, and water spurted from her mouth, as she began to cough. "Oh thank you God!' Wiley let out a prayer of relief. He picked Justice up, and walked back towards the park. She started moving and he stopped to lay her on the grass for a moment. Her eyes flew open and she looked wildly around.

"Justice?" He asked sitting beside her.

She coughed again and sat up "Where am I?" She caught sight of Wiley; dripping wet next to her and her eyes flew open.

"You're not dead, just so you know." Wiley said. "What were you thinking Justice!?"

To his surprise she jumped up and screamed. "No! I want to die! How dare you save me?" She tried to run.

As tired as he was, Wiley leapt to his feet and tackled her back to the ground. "No Justice no! You aren't going to die. You know why? Because I'm not about to let you kill yourself!" She struggled, but she was tired out and couldn't fight back very hard. She finally gave up and pounded her fists on the ground. "Just let me die, I don't want to live."

"God wants you to live!" Wiley exclaimed. "He led me to you, to find you and save you. Justice, we've just witnessed a miracle!" God had answered his prayer, and decided to give him a second chance at telling her the good news. He wasn't going to let a moment go to waste.

"No, I hate God. I don't believe in him!" She shouted over the storm.

"How can you hate him, if you don't believe in him Justice?" Wiley asked shaking his head.

Justice stammered. "I-I don't know. I don't believe in him but if he was real, I would hate him."

"Why? What's to hate?"

"He gave me a horrible life! He cursed me; he gave me hell on earth!" The rage in her eyes went so deep that Wiley could almost feel her pain.

"I don't know your life Justice, and I haven't been though all of the same stuff you have." He paused. "But I know God doesn't hate you, and he never intended things to be this way."

"Then why did they go this way huh?" Justice cried. Tears began rolling down her face and she choked out, "Why did he allow me to be born into a family that didn't want me?"

"The world's a bad place, it's sinful. I'm not going to defend it, but I am going to tell you that God wants the best for you and he wants to take away your pain...."

"You sound like Bill. I've heard it Wiley, I know what you're saying but I don't believe it. Miracles don't happen in my life and nobody would care about me enough to take away my pain." She cried again.

Wiley raised his voice slightly, to get her attention. "Justice would you stop, and wake up for a moment!?" he demanded. "What do you think God has been doing for you this whole week? He sent you to the Carters! They love you as their own daughter Justice! In fact, they have been looking for you none stop for the past two days. The whole church has been! The police have been alerted, and get this..." He paused. "Even Susan is looking for you and not just to place you in another foster home. Jane said that she sounded very upset and was trying to keep it together on the phone." He realized that she was quiet so he continued on. "I have been looking for you, and Justice it's been tough. I've been so worried! I prayed on the way to the park, that if God would just give me one more chance to share the good news with you, than I wouldn't let him down. Don't you see the miracle? He led me to you!"

Justice could feel her heart racing. This was unbelievable.

"Everybody's been looking for me?" She stammered.

"Yes the Carter's haven't stopped, I don't think they have slept, and man Vance is pretty torn up...as for Valley." He looked up at her, and his blue eyes stared right into her own. "I don't think Valley can make it without you. None of us can."

Justice started crying hard. Her whole body was shaking with sobs and she couldn't get the words that she wanted to say out. Wiley reached over and held her. She cried against him for several minutes. The lightning was flashing and the thunder was still crashing hard. The wind was cold and refused to stop blowing, but this was all ignored in these moments. The rain was still falling, but not in torrents as it had been before. Finally Justice pulled away, and looked up at him. "I never knew people could care about me so much." Her eyes were filled with disbelief and Wiley smiled. "I know. You see, you do mean something in this world. When you decided to kill yourself, you didn't realize that you would be hurting everybody else too."

Justice shook her head.

"God gave you this Justice, to show you just how important you are to him." He looked at her and let out a small smile. "If we all love you this much...imagine how much God must love you."

Her eyes went big, and she gulped, "I-I don't know. I never knew that he loved me...." Her voice trailed off.

"Justice, all he's wanted this whole time was for you to become..." He stopped for a moment and then added. "He wanted you to be his daughter."

Justice's eyes filled with tears again but she brushed them away. "You don't know how wonderful that sounds to me." Justice gulped, "Nobody has ever said that to me before. My own parents didn't want me...but your God would want me...just because he loves me?"

"Yes. He'll take over as your father in this life. That's what we call God you know, 'Our Father'."

Justice nodded. "Wow." She shivered and he realized for the first time, that they were still sitting on the wet grass of the park. The rain was falling harder now and Wiley suggested, "Why don't we find the Carters?" Justice remembered the whole situation. "Oh no. I don't want to face them right now. I can't. Not like this."

"Justice, they're so worried about you! We have to call them!"

Justice began to cry again. "No Wiley, nobody has ever seen me like this before. I don't want to face anybody else now."

"Okay, I have an idea." Wiley winked. They got in his car and headed off.

Justice sat on the couch wrapped up in a blanket. Wiley had taken her home to change into dry clothes, and then he drove her back to his house. He introduced her to his parents and they were so relieved that she had been found. Wiley had asked them to refrain from calling the Carters for just a couple more minutes, saying Justice needed some time. So they had and sat down in the living room with Wiley and Justice. Both of them were dry now, but were still glad for the blankets that they had around them. It had been pretty cold the last few hours.

Wiley looked over at Justice. She had calmed down a great deal and her hair was brushed away from her face and was starting to dry. A few stray tears would fall, here and there but they weren't angry tears.

"So how are you doing?" Wiley asked gently.

She laughed slightly. "Oh man, I'm crazy. Maybe Susan should place me in a mental hospital." She sounded more like her usual self when she said that and it made Wiley laugh back.

"Yeah well, that was pretty crazy."

"I know." She sobered. "I need to call the Carters."

"Do you want me to call them for you?" Mrs. Taylor offered a concerned look on her face.

Justice smiled. "Thank you, but no." She breathed in and let out a long breath pf air. "I need to do this." She winked at Wiley, and rose to get the phone.

Wiley's eyes lit up and he was proud of her. Justice returned with the cordless phone in hand and entered Jane's cell phone number. She sat back down on the couch, and looked at Wiley. "It's ringing."

"Hello?" Asked a grief-stricken voice on the other end. The sound of that voice made Justice want to cry again. It was so sad. Tears started to fall…

"Hello?" Asked the voice again.

"Jane…" Justice didn't need to say anything else.

"Justice! Oh thank God! Justice!" the voice was hysteric, and Justice only replied, "Yes it's me. I'm at the Taylor's house."

The phone was put on speaker and Justice could hear Bill too. "Justice! Stay on the phone! No wait, I have to call Vance, he's out somewhere…" Then she heard Jane say "But don't hang up!" Wiley heard that and suggested that he would call Vance on his cell phone. Justice told the Carters and they agreed. Justice could hear Valley yelling for the phone, so she could talk to Justice too. In moments the little girl picked up. "Justice?"

"Hey girl, it's me." Justice lost it then and started crying.

"Shh, don't cry Justice we're almost there." Valley announced.

Justice was touched by the little girl's kindness, and didn't know what to say.

The Carters stayed on the phone with her the whole time,

until they pulled up in the driveway. The car had barely parked, when Jane and Valley hopped out and ran for the door. Mrs. Taylor had been expecting them and she opened the door quickly for them. In moments, Justice felt herself being embraced by many people. Wiley had gotten in touch with Vance, and he pulled up right after the Carters. Bill came in with him and…was that Ryan? They all came up to her and hugged her tightly. Justice wept and they wept with her.

Questions spurted from every angel, and she answered the ones she felt like she wouldn't cry upon answering, and told them she would explain later, for the ones that would send her over the edge at the moment. The Carter's never scolded her for running away, they were just so happy to have her back. Justice had never known so much love, as she had this very night.

Chapter Fifteen
Justice for All

The sun shone brightly, and nobody would have known that this time a week ago, a raging storm took over. The air was cooler out, and it held promise of fall. Yes the summer was almost over, but the change was a good one. Justice smiled as she sat on the porch chairs out front. Jane accompanied her, as well as Susan. They were signing the necessary papers for Justice's adoption. It was true. Susan had called the family back that were planning to adopt Justice and told them that something had come up. Justice was already in the process of adoption. When Bill Carter had announced to Justice that he and Jane, as well as Vance, and Valley wanted to adopt her, she had leapt for joy. Susan had agreed to it, and when she saw Justice again. (Much to Justice's amazement), she cried. She wrapped her arms around her, and said that she would be more than happy to sign the papers. Justice had seen a side of Susan that she had never thought existed. She really did love her. Bill was right. The day had finally come when she realized how much Susan loved her. Now they were best buds, and it was a great feeling. The bitter anger that had nested in her heart all these years was gone, and although Justice knew that she would still suffer from it, from time-to-time, she knew whom to turn to. She had accepted Jesus that very day she was rescued. The things Wiley had said, and the love they all showed her, convinced her that they weren't lying. She now was adopted into Christ's family, and she had never known such a joyful feeling. She was part of a family at last! She realized that it didn't matter where she went now, because no matter what foster home she would be placed in, she would always be a part God's family. Of course when the Carter's announced their decision to adopt her, she was thrilled. She explained everything to the Carter's over the course of the week, and they all understood. Some things were painful to talk about and they all cried, while other storied were funny, and they laughed.

It really had been a time of great joy this week.

"Justice." Susan called over to her, shaking her back to the present. "Want some lemonade?"

In all of her life, she had never been offered lemonade by Susan. It was funny. "Sure." Justice smiled, and accepted the glass Susan handed her.

"Okay this is the last one." Jane got ready to sign, and the rest of the Carters came out, as well as the Taylors, and Ryan. Ryan had been hanging out with the Carters lately, and was becoming a little fond of them as well. Justice found that Ryan and Vance got along pretty well, so they had been doing some stuff.

"Okay Hun, do the honors." Bill encouraged.

Jane ceremoniously picked up the pen, and signed her last signature. Everybody clapped, and cheers went all around.

"Well, you're officially free of me." Susan smiled at Justice.

"And just when we were getting along." Justice laughed.

Susan laughed back. "So how did I do this time huh? Think you'll stay with this family for a while?"

Justice winked. "You actually did good this time." Susan clapped her hands with pleasure.

After that little ceremony, they had some desert.

They all sat around the table in the dining room, and Justice knew it was a special occasion. They never ate in the dining room! She was at the head of the table, as the guest of honor, and she had never felt so important. She looked at all of the loving faces around her, and let herself smile. *Thank you father. You've shown me love, and I know you'll always be there for me. I won't run from you ever again.* Justice prayed silently in her head.

After that, Wiley asked if she would like to go on a walk with him. Justice agreed eagerly. She had wanted to tell him something, and now seemed like the perfect time. The sun was shining, the air was cool, and the breeze was gentle. Justice breathed in a breath and sighed contentedly.

"Beautiful day huh?" Wiley asked.

"Yeah it is."

"I just had to get outside you know? I can't stand being indoors on a day like this."

Justice agreed. Then a thought struck her. "Wiley, how did you know that I would be at that park?"

Wiley smiled. "I like to take pictures of storms, and so I headed to the park. It was a God-thing that I found you there."

"Wow. It sure was." Justice nodded. She stopped and waited for Wily to stop. He did, and turned towards her.

"I never said thanks for saving my life. If it weren't for you, I would have died. "Justice stared into his blue eyes that had made her giddy the first time she had seen him.

His smile was warm as he said, "Well, I've been thanking God all week that he led me there. I don't know what I would have done if you died. "He suddenly grew serious. "Just promise me that you'll never do something that crazy again, okay?"

"I promise." Justice smiled up at him.

Suddenly he bent down and kissed her cheek. Instantly she felt her face heat up, and she knew without needing a mirror, that her face was red. Inside she glowed with warmth, and she couldn't wait to tell Jane about it later. Jane seemed to enjoy teasing her about Wiley, and now something else would be added to the list.

Wiley smiled at her red face. Just then Justice heard footsteps behind her, and Vance plowed into her, nearly knocking her over. "Tag, your it!" He yelled and sprinted past her. Okay, so some things she would need to get used to. Like Vance running into her, after a nice little moment with Wiley… but hey, what were brothers for?

The next day, Justice was made officially adopted, because all of the paperwork had been turned in. She would always remember the big deal that was made of it. They went to their church and had a big party. Everybody was invited, and then Justice was asked to come to the front of the room, where the Carter's showed Justice her certificate of adoption.

"Now we have a new family member, and her name is Justice Carter!" Everybody clapped, as Bill said those words. She liked the sound of her new name. Justice Carter.

Bill led them in a prayer after that, and everybody bowed their heads. "Father we just thank you for Justice, and we are so blessed to have her with us. Please help Jane and I to be good parents and to teach her about you…" The prayer went on for a couple seconds longer and ended with an 'amen'.

Then Justice walked outside for a little peace, and prayed her own little prayer. She thanked God for showing her *justice*, just like her name, and prayed that there would be *justice* for all, whom felt that wrong had befallen them. Jane walked outside and said, "Hey you, I was wondering where you went off to. What are you doing out here?"

Justice turned around and smiled. "Just praying."

Jane put an arm around her shoulders and asked, "What are you praying about?"

"I'm thanking God for the new family he's given me."

Jane smiled at that, and led her back inside to be with the rest of their family. A family that she would be apart of for the rest of her life. "That's great honey."

She loved God, she loved the Carters, and she knew that she would never hate again.

"Yeah," she said, and walked inside with her new mom.

No matter what happened in her life Justice would never forget what God had given her. He gave her life, a family and hope. In the most trying time He showed her where hope can be found. Justice smiled, and walked in to greet her new family.

THE END

This is a fictional story about adoption.
Summary:
Sixteen-year-old Justice Clarks is a name that nobody wants to hear! She's one of the most infamous foster kids around. Her constant fits of rage, sneaking out, getting drunk, and running away causes her social worker, Susan, to dispair. Every attempt at placing Justice Clarks with a family has been disasterous. Can there be any hope?

The Carter's are a different kind of family. Still healing from the death of their beloved daughter, the pastor, his wife, and two children contemplate adoption. Along comes Susan with an unexpected request. The Carter's are about to meet Justice, but is this what they had in mind? As for Justice, this is another foster family, and probably another painful disappointment—Her time is running out. One more let-down will push her over the edge. Susan fears that a mental hospital may be the only place Justice will ever call home.

This is a story of hope, healing and the belief in something greater than our pain.

Also available from PublishAmerica

SHINE AND INSPIRATIONS
by Tiffiney Rochelle Bradley

Shine and Inspirations is a text designed to teach humanity the purpose and role of prayer in everyday life. This book seeks to deepen believers' insights and understanding of how a continual prayer life will serve to strengthen the soul of believers and equip them in remaining encouraged while in the midst of life's stormiest situations.

Another book, entitled *Inspirations*, a collection of Christian testimonies, is included. Many of these touching testimonies explain how prayer served to stabilize and/or uplift those who testified out of situations such as HIV, severe physical illnesses, single parenthood, and hunger. Read, enjoy, and forever be inspired as you connect with the Spirit of Christ, which will enable you to Shine.

Paperback, 198 pages
6" x 9"
ISBN 1-4241-8489-4

About the author:

Shine and Inspirations came to life out of my call to serve the Lord, and my passion to help people. Prayer is having an intimate conversation with God. Having a Master's degree in Communications and having served in the field of education has been quite fulfilling, but publishing *Shine and Inspirations* has also been fulfilling, if not more so. What could be more exciting for a communicator and a servant of the Lord than helping others experience a dimension in Christ that I have already experienced.

Available to all bookstores nationwide.
www.publishamerica.com